# The Family Way

# The Family Way

LAURA BEST

NIMBUS
PUBLISHING
— NIMBUS.CA —

# Praise for the Cammie series

## THE FAMILY WAY

"*The Family Way* is a compelling story about a dark but significant past that few Nova Scotians are alive to remember. Laura Best's intriguing narrative shines a light on the challenges of a family exposed to the devious couple who ran the Ideal Maternity Home.... Best weaves the tragedy of the Butterbox Babies throughout the plot to captivate readers from start to finish. Enlightening history ideal for middle-grade readers."
–**Bette Cahill**, award-winning journalist and author of *Butterbox Babies*

"*The Family Way* illuminates a dark chapter in Nova Scotia's history for young readers with sensitivity and care. Laura Best has a gift for making the past feel vivid and near and her rural east coast settings like home, even for those who've never been."
–**Hadley Dyer**, author of *Johnny Kellock Died Today*

"This richly detailed historical novel explores issues of morality and prejudice when a young girl stumbles upon a secret of unimaginable horror. I enjoyed every page of this beautifully written story."
–**Valerie Sherrard**, author of *The Rise and Fall of Derek Cowell*

"Compelling characters and a pitch-perfect story about a young girl with a hardscrabble life, a bossy mother, and one good friend. As events draw Tulia ever more deeply into the ominous underside of the Ideal Maternity Home, she journeys from denial to horrified acceptance—and courageous action."

**–Jill MacLean,** Ann Connor Brimer Award–winning author

## CAMMIE TAKES FLIGHT

*Nominated for the 2018 Silver Birch Award*
*Best Books for Kids and Teens list (starred choice)*

"Compellingly written and original in concept."
**–Canadian Review of Materials,** *highly recommended*

"In this touching sequel to *Flying With a Broken Wing*, author Laura Best continues Cammie's story, this time focusing more on her search for identity and her quest to confront the ghosts of her past…. A moving story that holds multiple surprises for Cammie and for readers."
**–Atlantic Books Today**

## FLYING WITH A BROKEN WING

*Bank Street College Best Books of 2015*

"A charismatic protagonist and captivating setting make *Flying with a Broken Wing* a worthwhile read."
**–CM Magazine**

Nimbus Publishing Limited
3660 Strawberry Hill St, Halifax, NS B3K 5A9
(902) 455-4286 nimbus.ca

*This novel is a work of fiction. Names, characters, places, and incidents are either the product of the author's imagination or are used fictitiously.*

NB1518

Printed and bound in Canada
Editor: Penelope Jackson
Editor for the Press: Whitney Moran
Design: Heather Bryan


Library and Archives Canada Cataloguing in Publication

Title: The family way / Laura Best.
Names: Best, Laura (Laura A.), author.
Identifiers: Canadiana (print) 20200386794 | Canadiana (ebook) 20200386808 |
ISBN 9781771089340 (softcover) | ISBN 9781771089395 (EPUB)
Classification: LCC PS8603.E777 F36 2021 | DDC jC813/.6—dc23

Nimbus Publishing acknowledges the financial support for its publishing activities from the Government of Canada, the Canada Council for the Arts, and from the Province of Nova Scotia. We are pleased to work in partnership with the Province of Nova Scotia to develop and promote our creative industries for the benefit of all Nova Scotians.

MIX
Paper from
responsible sources
FSC® C013916

# Publisher's Note on Language

*The Family Way* is set in a time—the 1930s—and a place—rural Nova Scotia, Canada—when hurtful words used to describe certain members of a community would have been common. In this book, the word "Indian" is sometimes used by white characters to refer to the character of Finny Paul, who is Indigenous. This word is both offensive and hurtful, and is an example of overt racism. Today, we use more respectful words like Indigenous, Mi'kmaq, or First Nations.

The writer and publisher include the term to accurately reflect the time and place in which this story is set, as well as to authentically demonstrate the difficult realities for Indigenous peoples at that time. We hope its inclusion does not cause any hurt to readers.

We see this as an opportunity for discussion, and for learning, as we Settler Canadians make a conscious effort to reckon with our own racist histories and become better allies to the Indigenous peoples who have lived here for thousands of years.

*For my dear little Charlotte*

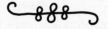

# Prologue

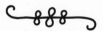

If it wasn't for Finny Paul I'd have spent a lonely childhood at the old farmhouse in East Chester, just Ma and me. Ma seemed married to that treadle sewing machine of hers, closed up in the sewing room for hours on end as she stitched up outfits for paying customers. Not to mention all the diapers and gowns Mrs. Young put in orders for on a fairly regular basis, as if Ma wasn't entitled to having some free time away from the maternity home. Ma was driven like that, always taking on more, determined to never be beholden to other people the way she was right after Daddy died.

I'm not by nature an overly curious person, but it was hard for me to mind my own business when Finny was around. He had a way of drawing me into his schemes. I should state that I rarely went along willingly. Ma would have boxed my ears for sure if she ever found out. In Finny's mind there were some serious wrongs taking place at the maternity home just down the road from us and no matter how hard I tried to convince him otherwise, he wouldn't give in. I'd plead for Finny to leave good enough alone. All I wanted was for life to go along smoothly until I was old enough to move as far away from East Chester as I could.

While Finny's curiosity often annoyed me, without him I surely would never have found out the truth about Becky. For certain Ma never intended on letting it pass her lips. She'd have gone to her grave without telling me what really went on. And as much as I'd always disliked deceit, what started out as this family's secret grew over time until I was the one left with the biggest secret of all.

# Part One

1939

# Chapter One

"It's time to toughen your knuckles, Tulia May, there's a mound of dirty diapers waiting for us. Hurry along so we can get an early start." Ma stood in front of the hallway mirror and quickly fixed her hair. I could tell she'd been fretting over the amount of grey she'd been seeing lately even though she hadn't said anything. Seemed to me she never gave it a second thought until someone in town mistook her to be my grandmother. You see, Ma was older than everyone else's mother, her turning forty-nine the year I was born. While I would never have said a word about it to Ma, her age did little for my popularity among my school friends—not that I ever cared about being popular. That was more Becky's department than mine. By the time I came along Ma was a grandma herself. If that's not enough to make your kid a laughingstock at school, I don't know what is.

I let out a big sigh. "Oh Ma, it's a Saturday, not to mention summer vacation. I've got things to do."

"And you've got six more weeks in your summer vacation to do whatever those things are," she scoffed. "It's not going to kill you to help out in a pinch. You've helped out plenty of times in the past. I don't need to remind you that Mrs. Young has been good to us."

Ma was right about that. Before she started working out at the maternity home, we didn't have two cents to jingle on a tombstone. Mrs. Young even gave Ma the old jalopy that had been sitting out at the maternity home rusting away. She hired John Burke to get it up and running and even gave Ma some driving lessons to get her started. Regardless of all that, I have to say that scrubbing stinky diapers was pretty low on the list of things I wanted to do on a Saturday.

"The quintuplets can wait another day," Ma stated as she reached for her handbag.

A new batch of magazine clippings had arrived in the mail yesterday from Aunt Maggie. I was anxious to get them pasted into my scrapbook and Ma knew it. She didn't approve of me saving pictures of the world's most famous babies, although she did allow me to glue a double-page magazine photo of them on my bedroom wall. That was only because it covered the crack in the plaster and helped keep the cold from coming in during the winter.

"It's unnatural, the way they've got them penned in like animals," Ma said, a sentiment she'd repeated more than once since I'd started the scrapbook.

"*Quintland*, Ma, they happen to live in Quintland, and I bet you'd be looking at them too if you were there." By the photos I'd seen, the quintuplets didn't want for a thing—something not many could say during the Depression years. I didn't see what the big deal was. Ma just liked to be difficult.

"Magnolia had no business getting you hooked on all that," she added as if there was something criminal in my having a pastime.

"I've got to have something to do," I shot back. It wasn't as if I had anything resembling a social life. Most of the girls at school were standoffish and kept to themselves. You were only allowed into their group if you were friends with Catherine Haley, whose popularity could only be attributed to the fact that she wasn't someone you wanted to cross. I'd grown up with most of them and although I never found a best friend among them, I got along with all of them fairly well. It was a matter of never taking sides, of being impartial during their disputes, knowing that eventually all disagreements would be forgotten.

The unpopular girls spent their time jumping through barrel hoops to impress Catherine and hoping to get invited into her group. I managed to remain on the outside of both groups and for the most part was ignored. I did sometimes hang out with Hope Steward and Marlee Fuller, who'd been told in no uncertain terms that they'd never be invited into the popular group, something they spent their time lamenting. I'd commiserate with them on the odd occasion but truthfully I didn't care about that foolishness.

"There's plenty to do around the house if you're looking for a pastime. Now don't drag your heels, Tulia," said Ma, waiting to close the door behind us.

Up until a year ago I used to go to the maternity home every Saturday morning. But then something came over Ma and suddenly she didn't want me tagging along as often. She claimed she didn't want me influenced in a bad way because *the maternity home was no place for impressionable young girls to be hanging out*—Mrs. Jefferson's words, not Ma's. Thanks to that comment, Ma started leaving me home with a long list of chores that needed to be done. But that Saturday Ma was in a real bind. It had been a drizzly, rainy week. While she was able to dry some of the diapers on makeshift lines in the laundry room, the diaper situation would soon be dire. That didn't even count all the gowns and sheets that needed washing. The nursery being filled with babies most of the time meant there was an endless need for all these things.

An unpleasant odour met us in the doorway when we entered the laundry room. If people think babies smell good they should try washing mounds of dirty diapers for a change. We carried water and filled up the washing machines. When Ma first came to work at the maternity home, Mrs. Young bought another washing machine to keep up with all the laundry that was accumulating from the growing population of babies. Ma being Ma, she still insisted on each diaper being scoured on the scrub board before putting them into the machines for a second go around. No one would ever say that Naomi Thompson didn't make those diapers down at the maternity home sparkle.

Holding my breath, I pushed several diapers into the washtub and started scrubbing while Ma put a load of gowns and crib sheets into the washing machines. She had been right about one thing: my knuckles could have stood some toughening up. It didn't take long before I felt a sting as two round blisters formed on my right hand.

"If you were using the scrub board the right way that wouldn't happen," she sniffed.

"Why can't we just throw them in the washing machine?"

"Because diapers need special care. Now just keep scrubbing."

Late morning, I reached for the last pile of dirty diapers with a sense of relief. Ma hadn't exaggerated—the mounds had been high—but the work was going better than I'd expected. I might still have time to paste some pictures in my scrapbook when I got home. The wash basket was rounded up with a stack of newly laundered diapers. Ma let out a soft grunt as she picked it up. I pushed the last of the dirty diapers into the washtub and reached for the laundry soap. The four long lines of diapers were filled every morning. In the afternoon some of the girls at the home did the ironing and folding. This was all subject to change depending upon the weather, of course. It was an endless task, all those diapers to keep clean.

As the washing machines continued to churn, I made up nonsense words to go along with the swish, swish, swishing that was vibrating a steady rhythm in my head. I was down to scrubbing the very last diaper in the pile when I heard a commotion outside. I hurried to the door in time to hear Ma shouting. A string of snow-white diapers was flapping in the breeze directly behind her. The empty wash basket was on the ground by her feet, and she looked as though she was ready to put up her dukes.

"You'd best hightail it out of here before I get a stick," she said. When a tall, thin figure disappeared through the hardwood trees behind the maternity home, it didn't take me being a genius to see why she was irritated. The sight of Finny Paul always ruffled her feathers—him being Evy's son and all.

"Oh Ma, he's not up to anything," I called out from the doorway. "Just leave him be."

"The nerve of his kind hanging around here," she sputtered as she breezed in past me with the empty laundry basket now resting on her hip. "Mrs. Young would have something to say about *that* if she knew."

"Maybe he has a reason for being here—ever think of that? And now you just chased him off so I guess we won't know, will we?"

"I very much doubt he has a reason for being here," she said, filling the washing machine one last time. "What business would he have to be out here? Up to no good, is what. Say what you want, but you can't trust those people. I've seen enough in my time to know." The diaper in her hands made a loud snap as she shook it out.

Ma's comments annoyed me. It wasn't that she knew anything about Finny Paul, only that his mother left my older brother, Bobby, years ago to marry Nelson Paul. And still, whenever Ma got together with Aunt Maggie, she'd dredge it all up again. You'd think she'd be over it by now.

"Imagine leaving a Thompson for a Paul," she'd say, which had little to do with Nelson stealing Evy's heart and a lot to do with him being a full-fledged Indian. Ma never fooled me.

When the last of the diapers were churning in the machine, there came a loud scuffing of feet on the stairs above us. Seconds later someone yelled down into the laundry room.

"It's Donna, Mrs. Thompson...the baby...her baby's coming."

"Well, stop your blathering and go fetch Mrs. Young," she called back, looking as baffled as what I was feeling.

"I can't...Mrs. Young's not back yet."

"Well, go get Mr. Young, then." I could see that Ma was getting ready to protest. Her job was to do laundry, not help deliver babies.

"I don't know where he is...Mrs. Thompson, please, Donna needs help. She needs it now. She can't wait for someone to fetch Mr. Young." Panic was building in the girl's voice. Seconds later, the upstairs thumped with the sound of more footsteps. Next came another sound resembling that of a wounded animal.

I grabbed fast to Ma's arm. Someone had to help. "Ma," I whispered in desperation. Sending me a look of annoyance, she sighed and shook my hand off.

"Finish up here, Tulia, and then go home," she ordered. "Don't wait for me. You hear? You go on home."

I nodded, relieved down to the tips of my toes. The last thing I wanted was to witness a baby being born, especially a baby that was capable of bringing about such horrifying sounds.

Drying her wet hands on her apron, Ma pushed back her shoulders and marched up the stairs like an army soldier. If she had no idea how to help bring a baby into the world, her body language gave no indication. I hung out the last of the diapers as quickly as I could. Donna's muffled screams could be heard all the way out by the clothesline. I tried to block out the noise. It wasn't an easy thing to do. As I was pinning the last diaper on the line, Mrs. Young's car came up the drive. I breathed in a sigh of relief. Everything would be okay now. Mrs. Young was here.

# Chapter Two

I met Finny Paul the fall I started school. Even with the long walk, Ma agreed to let me go, but only because I begged her constantly, and because Becky promised she'd look out for me.

"Stick with me," she said that first day when she saw the worried look on my face. I was fine up until the moment I saw that red building in the distance. "I won't let anything happen to you. We're family, and family always sticks together. Promise." She squeezed my hand as we walked into the schoolhouse and every day for the first month she made that same promise. Becky was in the tenth grade at the time and the sibling closest to me in age. She was also the most responsible Thompson in our family, which worked in my favour.

For the first few years I paid little attention to the boy who sat at the back of our one-room school. "Go back to the reservation," some of the older boys would shout at him in the schoolyard. At five years old, I had no idea what that meant. He was just a boy the other kids sometimes made fun of, and someone I instinctively knew enough to keep my distance from. Finny had a smart mouth on him and would sometimes crack jokes during class. There were times when you couldn't help but laugh, but he wasn't the only one. Miss Forrester was constantly telling him and the other boys to settle down and pay attention or else run the risk of failing a year. It was a threat none of them ever seemed to take seriously.

Although we technically met the first year I started school, it wasn't until four years later, when we both landed out at Lancaster's dump one Saturday in early September, that we became friends. If Ma ever found out where I went those Saturday mornings she'd have twisted my ear up tight and led me all the way to my bedroom, where I'd have been made to spend the next ten years of my life—when I wasn't in school, that is. That was back when Ma thought nothing of letting me head into town on weekends to hang out at the general store. Mr. Jefferson would sometimes hire me to sweep his floor in exchange for some humbugs or Chicken Bones. Little did Ma know that a trip to Mr. Jefferson's most often started with a quick stop off at Lancaster's.

If it wasn't for the fact that me and Finny spied the same bicycle one Saturday morning at the dump, I don't think we'd have ever become friends.

"Finders keepers!" yelled Finny as we both dashed toward the rusted relic. Finny was digging his feet in. I already knew he was fast from watching him on the playground. I'd hungered for a bicycle for as long as I could remember. It wasn't as if they were a dime a dozen in East Chester back in those days. It was safe to say that Ma would never scrape up the money for even a second-hand one. In Ma's eyes, a bicycle was something we could live without. Food and clothing, on the other hand, were not. If we had a hundred dollars to spend, Ma wouldn't budge an inch in that regard.

A burst of energy surged inside me as I raced toward the bicycle for all I was worth. Luckily, I was handier to the bike when we both saw it sticking out of the rubble or I'd have never stood a chance. I was positive that this was my one and only chance of ever owning one. We reached that old bicycle at the same time, both clamping on tight with no thoughts of letting go. I latched on to the back tire, and Finny had hold of the handlebars. I gritted my teeth and was preparing to start a tug-of-war, but then Finny said, "Why don't we just share it?"

It seemed almost unthinkable that a boy, a boy who was older than me, someone I hardly knew, an Indian boy at that, would come up with such an outlandish idea. Debating his proposal, I quickly decided it wasn't such a bad plan after all. Besides, he was bigger than me and could have taken it for himself without there being a thing I could have done about it. It seemed a decent thing for him to suggest. Not only had the bicycle seen better days, if it required any work to get it up and running—which, by the looks of it, I was fairly certain it would—any skills I had would be useless. There wasn't a mechanical bone in my nine-year-old body.

Finny said all it needed was to have the front rim straightened and a fresh coat of paint, maybe the chain greased, and right away I could tell he knew a lot more about getting it operational than I did. We later learned both inner tubes were in need of repairing, but Finny's older cousin had a tube-patching kit. In the end, even that wasn't a problem. We painted it bright yellow. Neither of us was partial to the colour, but as we soon found out, beggars don't get to be choosers. It was the only can we could find at the dump with enough paint to do the job.

Once the bicycle was fixed up as good as it could get without us asking for some adult help, we called it the Incredible Bee. It wasn't perfect, but perfect isn't always what you think it's going to be. Finny showed me what to do and I learned to ride that bicycle in two short days. We had hours of fun with the old relic until the day Griff Parker backed over it with his logging truck. But the Incredible Bee, that was the start of my friendship with Finny Paul.

There was little breeze as I headed for home that afternoon. I wondered how long Ma would be gone. Would she stay until Donna's baby was born? Instead of going straight home the way Ma told me, I turned down the road to Lancaster's dump. I'd heard some horrible sounds inside the maternity home, right frightening they were, and the last thing I wanted was to go home to an empty house. I secretly hoped I might find Finny Paul out at the dump. Although I hadn't been there since last fall, I knew he still went quite frequently. We used to spend a lot of our Saturdays sifting through other people's garbage, not that Ma would approve of my bringing something home from Lancaster's. Evy on the other hand was more than happy to make use of the things we found. But lately the dump wasn't holding the same interest for me. I was finding other things to occupy my time, my scrapbook being one of them. And there was this cute boy who occasionally came in with the New Ross freighters. I'd seen him at Jefferson's store a time or two. He was Jim Merry's boy and they sometimes stopped out at the maternity home. I'd been trying to think up ways to get his attention.

I raced down the road as a shot echoed in the distance and I wondered if Finny was target shooting again. My stomach rumbled. Hard to feel like eating with all the commotion that had been going on that morning. To tell the truth I'd forgotten all about eating. The sandwiches

Ma brought were still sitting on the table in the laundry room, untouched. Now I was wishing I'd thought to bring one with me.

I found Finny sitting on a big rock, cradling his father's .22 in the crook of his arm.

"Thought you might be here," I said, taking a place beside him on the boulder.

"Looks like you've been put through the wringer, Tulia....Get it—wringer?" he said, elbowing me gently in the side. He was smiling, the way he always did when he thought he'd come up with something clever to say. He was a good-looking boy with dark hair and eyes but that was as far as my interest in Finny Paul went. He was more like an older brother to me.

"You've got no idea, Finny, no idea whatsoever." I was eager to put the events of the morning behind me.

"Your Ma sounded plenty sore today," he said, still smiling.

"I'd think you'd be more careful. You know what Ma can be like, and Mrs. Young's not about to put up with trespassers...these days especially. What were you doing out there, anyway?"

"Look, there goes a big one!" Finny raised the .22 just as a large rat scurried out from behind a pile of garbage. Since I'd long ago learned to despise these creatures for sneaking into our barn at night and stealing the baby chicks, I didn't mind watching them tumble over in the dirt. Taking careful aim, he pulled the trigger. The air rang out from the shot as the bullet ricocheted off a piece of rusted metal and the rat disappeared into the garbage.

Finny looked back at me, serious in a way I didn't often see with him. "There's something fishy going on at that maternity home, Tulia. If the right people knew," he said, now resting the gun across his lap. I was hoping he wouldn't mention the maternity home at all. I gazed into Finny's dark eyes. It wasn't as if anyone in East Chester would listen to what he had to say. A lot of folks thought he should be living out on the reservation with his own kind. I'd seen the way some of the boys at school treated him. I used to wonder why Miss Forrester didn't tell them to stop.

"The Youngs were found not guilty a few months ago," I reminded him. There had been a trial and it was all folks talked about for a time. Finny had been so sure the Youngs would be thrown in jail. He'd read everything that was printed about the case. Maybe it was wrong, but I worried they'd get closed down and Ma wouldn't have a job. Not that Ma ever whispered a word about any of that to me. She seldom spoke about anything that went on at the maternity home. What little bit I knew came from Finny Paul, and most times I'd tell him to keep whatever gossip he'd heard to himself. Ma said it was up to the courts to decide. "I don't want you gossiping about this to anyone, Tulia," she instructed.

A crow cawed from the branches of the maple trees, breaking the awkward silence that had settled between us. There were things I could have said to Finny Paul that day, things I'd seen and heard over the years Ma had worked there. But something prevented me from opening up. *Why stir up a hornet's nest?* Ma used to say.

Finny wasn't one to be discouraged easily. "You may as well know, I'm planning to find out the real truth, Tulia," he said. His jaw was set with determination. "I'll go to the authorities if I have to."

"But what if they get shut down?" I said, suddenly on the defensive. What about all the people who depended upon the Youngs and the business they brought to the area? What about Ma and me? "The judge let them off." I wasn't sure why I needed to remind him of this.

"Well, judges make mistakes." I wished Finny would drop all this. "Your ma must have seen things." If Finny Paul thought I was going to help him shut down the maternity home, he'd better have another think coming. I looked back at the pile of garbage and forced a tiny smile. I jumped to my feet.

"You'll get that rat next time," I told him. I heard Finny hollering after me but I didn't stop and turn around. I'd promised Ma. I needed to get home.

I let out a gasp when I saw Ma's car parked in the driveway. I hadn't been expecting to see it. I'd heard stories about how long it took for babies to be born. Preparing myself for a blasting, I gingerly opened the front door. I was comforted to hear her treadle machine purring away. I hurriedly ate some bread and molasses to fill the hollow spot in my stomach. Ma would soon be starting supper. Taking a deep breath, I climbed the stairs to her sewing room. It was time to face the music.

"I'm sorry, Ma," I started to say, but then stopped short when I saw what she was bent over the sewing machine stitching. I gasped. White gowns were used as burial shrouds for the babies that didn't make it. Ma looked up at me. Her eyes held a sad story but she didn't say a word. Neither of us did.

Flopping myself down across my bed, I couldn't stop the flow of tears. I swore right then and there that I would never have a baby when I grew up—never.

# Chapter Three

⸾ 888 ⸿

It was the first day of August, hot and sticky. We had gone into town that morning for groceries. Becky was sitting at the kitchen table when we got home. It wasn't like her to show up at the house without warning, and I let out a quick gasp at the sight of her. We hadn't seen her since Christmas, when she stayed for three whole days. On Christmas Eve we went for a walk under the starry winter sky, just Becky and me, and she whispered that she'd met someone special.

"Is he handsome?" I asked, knowing that someone as pretty as Becky wouldn't settle for a homely man.

"Of course," she said, and we giggled ourselves silly. Later, she made me pinkie swear not to tell Ma. The last time Becky had a beau, Ma insisted that she invite him home. The moment he stepped through the doorway she proceeded to question him about his parents, them being the owners of the local funeral home.

"I don't see how anyone in their right mind could stand to be around dead people all day," Ma blurted out between mouthfuls of mashed potatoes. His face turned bright red and Becky sputtered and coughed.

It seemed no coincidence that he never came back.

"Didn't you get my letter?" Becky said, looking up at Ma. Her blue eyes appeared eager for an answer.

Ma let out a grunt and reached for her apron. "Put the groceries away, Tulia," she said, briskly tying the apron strings behind her back. The air was thick with tension that I tried hard to ignore. I hurriedly reached into the grocery box and took out the bag of salt and placed it on the pantry shelf.

"Why didn't you write me back?" Becky continued with indignation while I took out the rest of the groceries and put them away. "Ma, I was talking to you," she added when Ma failed to answer her back.

"I think I know who you're talking to. I'm just wondering what the devil you're doing here in the middle of the week. Running back home, now that you got yourself in a fine mess?" Ma's face didn't give an inch and I couldn't figure out why she was so angry with Becky for showing up without warning. More importantly, what was this mess she was talking about? Ordinarily, she was pleased as punch to have Becky home with us.

"Do I have to have a reason to come home?"

"Don't expect me to fix this for you," snapped Ma as

she proceeded to measure out flour from the bin. "I've no fix left in me."

The next thing I knew, the two of them were in a shouting match and I was being ordered to my room. When I started to protest, Ma's foot clacked down on the hardwood floor. I hurried up the steps and flopped down onto my bed. Reaching for my scrapbook, I opened it while the words *irresponsible*, *disgraceful*, and *never expected* rang out from below me. Becky's words were a quiet rumble, sandwiched between her sobs and Ma's shouts. With all those words barrelling throughout the kitchen, I couldn't make out a thing Becky was saying. A door slammed and there came more feet stomping. Becky began to sob again. I was dying to know what was going on.

Thumbing through my scrapbook, I paused and admired one of the photos of Elzire Dionne looking down at her babies, each of them wearing a little white bonnet. It was an old picture that had resurfaced a few months ago as a commemorative to the famous quintuplets' fifth birthday in May. The picture made me wonder what could have been going through her mind. I couldn't imagine what it would be like to have five tiny babies to look after all at one time.

As the rowing in the kitchen continued, I set the scrapbook aside and started for downstairs. Someone had to break this up. By process of elimination, that someone would have to be me. I hurried into the kitchen all the while Becky and Ma were going at it like sparring tomcats. Before I could get a word out of me, I was met with an "Upstairs, Tulia May!" from Ma that nearly rattled the dishes on the shelf.

"Oh Ma, I'm twelve years old. You can't order me around like a child," I said, folding my arms in front of me. It was time I told her how it was.

"That's enough of your smart mouth, Tulia. Now, do as I say." The look on her wrinkled face told me she meant business. It was no time to be talking back.

"You shouldn't be arguing with Becky, is all," I said, lowering my voice. "They're going to hear you all the way to Chester Basin if you keep this up."

My words must have struck a note with Ma because just then her tone softened—but only a bit. "This doesn't involve you, Tulia May…. Now, do as I say, like a good girl."

Whatever Ma and Becky were arguing about was serious. I knew better than to say anything more. Hurrying back upstairs, I returned to my quintuplet pictures. I was only too glad for the distraction.

Aunt Maggie had got me interested in keeping a scrapbook. Last summer, she brought a whole stack of *Star Weekly* magazines with her when she came to visit. Ma accused her of unloading her garbage on us instead of tossing it in the trash where it rightfully belonged. I must have gone through those magazines a thousand times, reading the articles and choosing which photos to put in the scrapbook. I discovered all the souvenirs made in the quints' likeness and wondered how people could be buying them up during such hard times. Not only that, people were going to Quintland in droves every year to see the quintuplets first-hand through the glass observatory. I could hardly imagine being so lucky.

My favourite quint photo was taken at the farmhouse the summer the babies were born, with two gigantic strings of diapers flapping in the breeze. It reminded me of the maternity home down the road whenever I looked at it. If Canada thought the quintuplets went through a lot of diapers they should have seen what was hanging on the clotheslines out at the maternity home most every day.

"I guess it's just you and me," I said, taking up my position on the bed, the scrapbook spread out before me as I studied the photos again. By the time I closed the covers, Ma and Becky had retired to their respective corners. Becky spent what was left of the day holed up in her room, and Ma's old treadle sewing machine was humming up a storm. I had just started the dishes when Becky came into the kitchen. After dipping up a bowl of stew for her, I turned back toward the sudsy water.

"How long are you staying?" I asked.

"I'm not sure. I've got some things to figure out." She gingerly tasted the stew. A little while after their fight she'd been sick. I'd heard her retching into the washbasin.

I blamed Ma for upsetting her. With all the shouting that had been going on, no wonder she didn't feel well.

"What about your job?" I said. A strange look crossed Becky's face. She loved her job more than anything in the world. While I couldn't imagine what it would be like to bathe grown people for a living, or to help feed them like babies, I accepted Becky's choice with a sense of relief. If Ma had one daughter who had made something of herself she'd be satisfied. Besides, my future plans involved travelling. A trip to Quintland was first on my list. If growing up in rural Nova Scotia taught me anything, it was to appreciate what the rest of the world had to offer. I wasn't sure what that was, but I was looking forward to finding out.

The next evening Becky came into my room and sat at the foot of my bed. A lock of her blonde hair was hooked behind her left ear; the other side was dangling loosely. Her face looked pinched, her eyes were watery, and her nose was red. She was clutching a twisted-up hanky. She and Ma hadn't pulled off a row that day, but neither were they talking to one another. To tell the truth, I was enjoying the peace and quiet. With a quilt drawn around her, Becky looked cold even though she couldn't possibly be that late into summer. I was reminded of the time she came into my room after Daddy died. The house was filled with relatives and neighbours all talking loudly, which was why I'd gone off to be by myself. We'd played with the paper dolls Aunt Maggie had sent me that Christmas and neither one of us said a word to the other.

Reaching for my scrapbook, I began showing Becky some of the pictures.

"This one reminds me of the maternity home," I said when I came to the photo of the diapers flapping in the wind. She jumped to her feet and raced from my room, wailing like a baby. I thought about when I was little and the times I would go running into the safety of her arms when I was at school. It was never what she said that made me feel better, it was just her way of being. I stood in the middle of my room looking out at the open doorway, wondering if I should go after her. But I had no idea what to do or what to say. Turning, I went back to my scrapbook, deciding it was probably best to let her be.

## Chapter Four

⌐~888~⌐

The summer after Daddy died I got my first taste of travelling. That was the year me and Ma took the train to Ontario to visit Aunt Maggie and Uncle Art. I was ten years old. Ever since then I started dreaming of one day seeing the Rocky Mountains and the flat farming land out west, the rocky shores of Newfoundland and the red sands of Prince Edward Island.

The tickets couldn't have come at a better time. They helped distract Ma from moping around those first months after Daddy died. When she took them out of the envelope, she inspected them without saying a word. I snatched them off the kitchen table to have a look. I couldn't help wondering if Aunt Maggie hadn't thrown good money away by mailing them down to us. Ma wasn't the travelling sort. It wasn't as if she'd ever expressed an interest in going to Ontario when Daddy was alive, as many times as Aunt Maggie and Uncle Art tried to entice her into going.

"*You've got to see all the wonderful things there are in Ontario, Naomi,*" Aunt Maggie would say. The expression in her voice and the light in her eyes made me yearn to go in a way I'd never experienced before. I was dying to see Ontario for myself.

"*I can't leave Gilbert with all the work*" was always Ma's excuse. "*Besides, he wouldn't have the sense to come in out of the rain if I wasn't here to tell him.*"

But the summer after Daddy died she agreed to go. The first place Aunt Maggie took us to was Niagara Falls. As I stood staring down into the aqua-coloured water, I never wanted to go back to East Chester again. I cried when it was time to take the train back home.

They say the only cure for grief is action and that must be true. It wasn't until Aunt Maggie sent us the train tickets that Ma found a way out of her mourning. Daddy dropping dead right on the spot is what put Ma in the rocking chair; the mess he left behind is what kept her there for two whole months. While it's not nice to speak ill of the dead, the real truth was that when Daddy died, he left Ma with a bunch of bills and no way to pay them. *He must have thought he was going to live forever*—Ma's words, not mine.

Right after we came back from Ontario, Ma marched herself out to Mrs. Young's maternity home and took a job for the first time in her life. After that, she only mentioned Daddy's name in passing, like he was an endnote to a story she was telling and not someone she'd spent the past forty years of her life waiting on hand and foot. It was as if she'd packed away her old life and opened another box marked *New-fangled*. I don't think she shed another tear over Daddy being gone after that. She was just too busy for that, but busy was the way Ma liked it, even with all her complaints about not having any time to relax and enjoy life in her middle age.


For the next few days Becky and Ma seemed to have called a truce. They spoke only when necessary, but that was better than their previous shouting matches. Between Ma's stubbornness and Becky's sulking, it didn't look as though I was about to find out what was going on anytime soon. And then one evening while Becky and I were washing up the supper dishes, we heard Ma start up the car and head off down the road. I gave Becky a queer look and she shrugged her shoulders. It wasn't like Ma to drive off in the evening like that.

"Who cares?" she said, wiping a dinner plate and setting it on the shelf. We worked for a time in silence as I tried to come up with a subtle way of asking what was going on between them. I didn't want her angry with me, too.

"Ma's plenty annoyed," I said, handing Becky a pot to wipe.

"That's nothing new for Ma," said Becky, and I couldn't argue that point. "You know you'll have to watch out,

Tulia, else you'll be stuck looking after her once you're through school."

Her words jolted me. "I'm not staying in East Chester all my natural born days."

"That's what you think now, but I bet Ma's got other plans for you. She'll probably want you to take up sewing. She's awfully proud of the reputation she built up over the years."

"Yeah well, I've got my own plans," I said sharply.

"I hope those plans don't involve Finny Paul," she said, setting a dried pot on the table. My hands dripping dishwater, I gave Becky a light smack on the shoulder. How could she suggest such a thing? "You know how Ma feels about Evy," she added.

"Don't you mean how she feels about Indians and Evy marrying one?" I said, boldly.

"Indian or not, Finny's a boy and Evy's son—that's reason enough for her."

"Finny and me are just friends, and that's all it's ever going to be." She gave a shrug, like she wasn't totally convinced. "Besides, I want to travel," I said, confessing my secret desire.

"Good luck with that," Becky snorted. "Ma's going to keep you here until she's gasping her last breath."

Becky's words caused a feeling of near panic to rise in me. Being the last of twelve put me in a tough spot. My brothers and sisters had left home at a respectable age.

My brothers all moved out as soon as they turned sixteen with Ma's blessing. They scattered about the countryside like snowflakes in the wind. My sisters didn't move out until they were married, except for Becky, who went off to nursing school and made Ma the proudest person in all of East Chester.

I was wiping down the sideboard and Becky was sweeping the kitchen floor when Ma drove in. I jumped when I heard the car door slam, still haunted by the notion that I was never going to leave East Chester. Ma marched into the kitchen, taking up more space than I would have thought possible for someone her size.

"Tulia, upstairs...I need to speak to Becky alone," she said. Tossing the dishrag onto the sideboard, I let out a grunt. This ordering me upstairs was becoming a habit.

"Well, it's just you and me again," I said, flopping down across my bed. Annette, Emilie, Cecile, Yvonne, and Marie looked up at me from the pages of my scrapbook. Good thing I'd never grow tired of seeing their round little faces. I turned a few pages and noted that no one was shouting downstairs. As I continued to flip through the scrapbook, a sense of calm descended over me and I smiled. Perhaps Ma and Becky were working their problems out.

Two days later Becky was gone. When I asked Ma where she was, she told me to just never mind. "You ask too many questions, Tulia," she said, the spoon scraping against the sides of the pot as she quietly stirred the porridge that morning.

I sighed in frustration. "Is Becky back at the hospital? Can you at least tell me that?"

She spooned some oatmeal into a bowl and, setting the remainder onto the cupboard, she went for her jacket. "I'm going to be late," she said.

"Why won't you tell me what's going on, Ma? I've got a right to know."

Ma spun around, pointing her finger at me. There was fire in her eyes as she said, "Becky came home long enough to stir things up. Now she's gone, and everything's back to normal. Case closed. I don't want to hear another word about it. Do you hear me?"

And that was that. She left the house without saying another word.

# Chapter Five

The morning mist snaked along the cove until it discovered the place where me and Finny Paul were standing. In the sky, a faint yellow orb was burning its way through the haze. I knew once the sun finally broke through the fog would lift, but that could be hours away.

"We've been standing here long enough, Finny Paul. Let's just go. The fog's like pea soup and the mackerel aren't hardly biting."

Ma had left for town before nine that morning and wouldn't be gone long. She wanted to get an early start on account of the Merrys were planning to drop in for a visit later in the day. It wasn't that she knew them well, they were merely acquaintances, but Ma always expected things should go perfect whenever company came. She'd invite them for supper before they headed back to Tanner. That was a given. One thing that could be said about Ma, she knew what good manners were. A few weeks ago, I'd overheard Mrs. Featherstone telling Ma that the Merrys were hoping to adopt one of the babies out at the maternity home.

"The Merrys seem like nice people and Mrs. Young sometimes adopts babies out to the locals. So you never know. Too bad they weren't able to have another child of their own." Mrs. Featherstone's voice dropped. And if she thought she could squeeze some gossip out of Ma when she added, "They say Ethel nearly went off the deep end when she lost the last one," she was mistaken. Ma just looked up at Mrs. Featherstone and cleared her throat. I doubted she knew anything, anyway.

"I daresay having a baby in the house would be a challenge after all those years," said Ma. I wondered then if she was speaking from experience.

"Hopefully things will work out for them," said Mrs. Featherstone. She brought her head down close to Ma's and lowered her voice again. "That's if Mrs. Young doesn't charge them an arm and a leg like they say she does those rich folks from the States."

"I wouldn't know anything about that," Ma said, pulling back her shoulders. "I only do the laundry."

It would be nice having the Merrys stay for supper if their son, Beecher, was with them. But since Ma hadn't mentioned his name I knew he wouldn't be coming. I'd seen him several times at Jefferson's store. He even smiled at me once. Last year when I was hanging out laundry at the maternity home, Jim Merry's wagon came around back. Beecher smiled and waved. I returned his wave but nearly dropped the diaper I was pinning to the clothesline. I could have died from embarrassment.

"Hold your britches, Tulia," said Finny, throwing his line out into the cove. The spinner made a hollow sound as it hit the water and quickly sank.

"I didn't expect it would take this long," I said as he reeled the line in. I didn't even know how to cast a line the proper way, let alone what to do if I ever had something flipping and flapping on the other end of it.

"It wouldn't hurt you to give it a try for once in your life," he said. I shifted my footing on the rocks as the spinner sank beneath the water's surface again.

Ma thought the Merrys might enjoy a feed of fresh mackerel for supper. I hunted up Finny the day before and told him we'd need some fish for the next day. I brought along Pa's old fishing gear and a bucket like always. Little did Ma know that the fish we'd dined on all summer had been caught by Finny Paul. All those times I went fishing with Daddy when I was small, Ma thought I'd learned how to fish. She sent me out that first time and told me not to come home until I'd caught enough for supper. Luckily, I ran into Finny Paul and he filled my bucket. Ma was thrilled with the catch and Finny had been reeling in mackerel for us ever since.

"Why don't you just throw in your line, Tulia? If you catch something, I'll take it off for you." There were only two small mackerel flipping around the bottom of my bucket, hardly enough to feed us, let alone the Merrys. "At least make it look like you're fishing," he added. "In case someone sees us."

"There's not another living soul out here on this foggy morning, let alone someone looking to spread gossip about us," I retorted. But I knew Finny was partly right. If we were seen together it would be sure to reach Ma's ears before the week was out. But if we were both seen fishing, people would be less likely to care.

"Shucks, Tulia, what's your problem? You're always in a big hurry."

"Ma will soon be back and we've got company coming." I'd cleaned most of the floors the day before, but Ma wanted the kitchen freshly scrubbed before the Merrys arrived.

Finny stopped reeling and, tilting his head toward the cove, held his hand up to shush me.

"Listen," he said, quickly bringing in his line.

I didn't imagine he'd heard anything. It was his way of shutting me up. I was about to tell him he was just faking, because I couldn't hear a thing, when a creaking sound echoed through the heavy fog. It was a mournful noise that slowly increased in volume until it became obvious that the sound was someone rowing a boat. Setting our rods down we ducked out of sight, peeking through a clump of bushes to see who it was.

"Look—there he goes again," said Finny, pointing out toward the foggy cove.

"There who goes?" As we peered through the bushes, a shadowy silhouette materialized through the grey haze.

"Old Joe Lewis, one of the groundskeepers out at the maternity home. He rowed out one day when me and Trevor were fishing." The fog being thick like it was made it nearly impossible to discern exactly who was out there. I couldn't imagine Finny knew either.

"It's a free country last time I looked. Besides, that could be anyone out there," I said, although I couldn't deny the fact that Finny was better at knowing these things than I was. Still, what was the harm?

The boat stopped out on the water, rocking gently in the waves.

"It's Joe, all right," said Finny with altogether too much confidence. "Other people have seen him too."

"You've got to stop hanging out at the feed store or else stop repeating the gossip you hear. Maybe he's just out fishing—have you thought of that, genius?"

"Folks are talking about what all he's been doing for the Youngs."

"Things like what?" If Finny had something to say, he'd best spit it out. I wasn't one for jumping to conclusions.

"Babies have died, Tulia. A lot of babies. People are

talking about it." My heart jumped as I thought about the burial shroud Ma was stitching for Donna's baby the other day.

"That's enough, Finny." I didn't want to hear anything more. I reached for the bucket of mackerel. The Merrys would have to have something else for supper. "I don't know why I let you talk me into coming here in the first place."

"You're the one who wanted the mackerel," said Finny defensively. The sounds from across the water grew in intensity, rattles and thumps that drew our attention back to the cove. When the person out on the water picked something up from the bottom of the boat, my knees began to go weak. Even if I were under oath, I cannot say for certain what it was—only that it appeared to be some sort of neatly wrapped bundle. A small splash of water followed as whatever it was disappeared into the water.

"He must have weighed it down. You know—to make it sink."

"Weighed what down?"

"The babies—the ones that don't make it. Some of them get dumped in the ocean. To keep the authorities from knowing." I refused to think about Donna's little baby lying somewhere at the bottom of the cove. I shook my head in protest. Finny was just wrong.

"You should be writing your ideas down on paper, Finny Paul, not trying to invent some real-life mystery,"

I said, landing him a quick wallop on the shoulder. He squawked and pulled back.

"I can't help what they're saying," he said.

I wasn't interested in knowing who *they* were or how *they* would know such a thing. The very thought of it was ridiculous. Stomping my foot in the dirt, I looked at Finny.

"It's a horrible thing you're saying here, Finny Paul—a horrible, horrible thing. He could be throwing anything in them waters—anything. And who's to say that's Joe for certain? It could be anyone." I refused to go along with Finny's speculation on what we had just witnessed.

I grabbed my fishing rod and bucket. Turning to go back down the foggy trail toward home, I left Finny Paul on the water's edge and scrambled up over the cliff as fast as I could. As I reached the top, he called for me to slow down, his words marring what remained of that foggy morning air. Something restricted my breathing, as if a heavy weight was sitting on my chest. I gulped, swallowing back something so sinister I could barely think it into being. At twelve, there were surely many things in the world that I didn't understand, but Finny and I witnessing some heinous act was an idea I refused to entertain. It couldn't be, just couldn't be.

My feet moved clumsily along the well-worn path beneath me as I hurried down the trail deepened by fishermen's feet over the years. I should have heeded Finny's warning to be careful but was unable to stop the momentum building as my one foot moved in front of the other. When he called out once again for me to slow down, I missed the path and the ground beneath me began to crumble. I could feel myself coming dangerously close to the edge. I didn't have time to scream. My feet went out from under me and I squeezed my eyes tight. The fishing rod and bucket went flying. I let out a quick squawk as Finny grabbed me by the waist and pulled me back onto the path. We landed on our rear ends in the heather.

I could feel Finny's heart racing as I collapsed against his chest. Tears came next. I couldn't hold them back. I sobbed like a little child on that bluff with Finny Paul holding me in his arms. He produced a hanky and handed it to me, telling me it was all right. But if that was what all right felt like, I knew I was in deep trouble. Crying into the hanky, I couldn't make myself stop. We sat there on the path, Finny patiently waiting for me to pull myself together.

The morning sun peeked through the fog and a soft wind skimmed my cheeks. Out on the water, the boat and its owner silently retreated across the cove.

"I'm ready to go home now," I finally said. I was unable to force the words *thank you* from my trembling lips even though I was about as grateful to Finny Paul for saving my life as any one person could be. Finny helped me to my feet. The look on his face told me he had plenty on his mind, things I was sure I didn't want to hear. He started to say something, but I pulled in a breath of courage and spoke firmly.

"Finny, don't. Whatever it is you have to say, I don't want to hear it."

Ignoring my protests, he continued, "Tulia...I think you should know."

"Know what?" I said a little too loudly. I shouldn't have barked at him the way I did, but the look in his eye, the sound of his voice, jarred me to the core.

"I saw your sister Becky," said Finny, and a strange feeling leaped into my chest. Becky suddenly showing up at the house; Ma and Becky fighting; Becky leaving without a trace; Ma refusing to tell me where she'd gone—I hadn't mentioned any of that to Finny. How could he possibly know anything about Becky?

"Becky? Are you sure? Where?" I tried to sound calm.

He didn't answer right away. I could see the wheels turning as if he were trying to decide what to say.

"Tell me," I implored. "Where did you see Becky?" Why didn't anyone want to talk about Becky?

He looked out toward the water, then back at me. "You're not going to like this."

"Finny, please!" I was becoming annoyed by this time.

"Out at the maternity home," he said, not meeting my gaze.

A cold wind whipped across the cove and I shivered.

Swallowing hard, I could feel a large lump in my throat. My lips trembled but I wasn't about to start crying again. It was as if, in that moment, I'd been sucker-punched in the mouth.

# Chapter Six

⎯ 888 ⎯

I begged Finny to tell me all he'd seen. He hadn't a lot to say, only that someone who looked like Becky was hanging out laundry a few days ago. The maternity home was a busy place with all those girls coming and going. There could be any number of girls there who might resemble Becky from a distance. I asked him how far away he was from the clothesline.

"Shucks, Tulia, I wasn't carrying a ruler," he said.

"It doesn't make sense that Becky would leave her job to work at the maternity home," I said, thinking out loud.

"What if she's not just there to work?" Finny had a strange look on his face. He liked to think the worst.

"Of course she's working. I'm sure it's no big deal." Finny was always jumping to conclusions, something I was forever telling him not to do. He didn't know Becky the way I did; she was always thinking about some way to help others.

"I hope so," was all he said.

I'd barely made it home and was pulling my grass-stained dress up over my head when Ma's car came sputtering up the driveway. I was changed by the time she put it in park and was partway down the stairs when she opened the door.

"Bring in the groceries, Tulia. I haven't got all day," she said as she marched in through the door. She removed her hat and peeled off her jacket in record time, then hung both up on the rack. Her handbag she shoved onto the closet shelf. She hurried to the kitchen while I stood frozen, wanting to blab out what Finny had just told me about seeing Becky. Surely Ma knew. She worked out at the maternity home every day. But why be so mysterious about Becky working there? Was she ashamed that the daughter who had made something of herself left her good job at the hospital to help care for unwed mothers? It was the only explanation I was willing to consider. While Ma didn't mind taking a wage from Mrs. Young, she'd voiced her opinions about Lila Young's girls in the past, and not all of it was flattering. Ma could be a snob in that regard. It wasn't as if Becky was one of those wayward girls Lila Young brought into the maternity home. She just wasn't. Ma needed to lighten up and stop worrying about what people would think.

Then again, Finny could have been mistaken. It had been a long time since he'd seen Becky. Maybe the girl he saw only looked like Becky. I decided it was best to wait until I had more information before presenting it to Ma. If I was wrong I'd never hear the end of it.

I was brought back to my senses by a foot stomp and a sharp "Tulia May Thompson, get moving!"

"Okay, Ma," I said, hurrying for the front door. "We'll have to have something else for supper. The mackerel weren't biting. I only got two. They're in the sink." I could hear her sputtering from all the way in the kitchen as I went to get the groceries.

Ma hurried through the rest of the day, anxious in a way that made me wonder why. It wasn't as if the Merrys were considered important company; they were farmers from Tanner. She was certainly used to cooking for other folks. I'd seen her fix meals for as many as thirty for Christmas dinner. Not to mention that when Pete and his gang came out for supper, Ma was always in her glory. As well as being the best seamstress in these parts, Ma was also known for being an exceptional cook, something she took plenty of pride in. But then, everything Ma did was of high quality, which was why she always expected perfection from those around her—meaning me, mostly.

When the Merrys arrived, she welcomed them with open arms, offering them a broad-toothed smile that she usually reserved for folks like the Youngs and that government inspector who showed up at the home one day last month. We made our way through supper with the most polite conversations. Not that Ma didn't think good manners were important, because she did, but her behaviour was so overdone. There are only so many stiff smiles you can tolerate during one meal. While Mr. Merry sounded disappointed to learn that there'd be no mackerel for supper, he dug right into the chicken and dumplings Ma had prepared. Ma looked pleased when he complimented her cooking, telling her everything was top-notch.

"Isn't it, Ethel? Isn't this the best chicken and dumplings you ever ate?"

"Why yes, Jim. It certainly is." Mrs. Merry had a kindly face and I thought she'd probably make a good mother to some poor baby at the maternity home. That was, if Mrs. Young let them adopt one. I even started to feel sorry for her not being able to have another baby after Beecher was born.

There were pleases and thank yous galore, something that was always sure to impress Ma about company. Although I thought she seemed a bit on edge as she spooned out the apple crisp, commenting on how the yellow-transparent apples made the best crisp.

"Oh yes, they certainly do," agreed Mrs. Merry. Their politeness was so exaggerated that I had to wonder whose benefit it was for. It was as artificial as the faded silk flowers Mrs. James had stuck out in the planter on her doorstep for the past two summers. Ma asked me to please pour the tea, and by the time the last morsel of apple crisp was being scraped from the plates, I was politely told to excuse myself from the table.

"Didn't I hear you say that you owed Magnolia a letter?" Ma added.

"But the dishes," I protested—but only slightly, lest I'd get stuck doing them all by myself. Ma always wanted them done right up after a meal.

"Don't worry about the dishes this time. Just run along," said Ma impatiently. Not that she fooled me for a moment. I could tell she wanted me to make myself scarce so that she could discuss something with the Merrys. I guess Ma wasn't as opposed to gossiping as I'd thought.

Half-miffed at Ma for treating me like a child, I headed for my room. Ma was right, I did owe Aunt Maggie a letter; I just didn't appreciate her using that as an excuse to be rid of me. As I started toward the steps, an idea struck me and I decided to make a quick detour before heading to my bedroom.

Grabbing my jacket from the rack, I hurried off to the maternity home. Ma could discuss whatever she wanted with the Merrys. I had other, more important things to do. Still, it was highly annoying. It wasn't as if I was a child that needed shielding from the world. She had never kept secrets from me in the past. Why start now?

A warm August breeze met me right outside the door. The sun was low in the sky. I had no idea how long the

Merrys would be staying and I didn't care. There was only one thing on my mind: I needed to get to the truth before I allowed myself to suppose things that just weren't right and blame Ma for keeping secrets. I owed her that much. There was no sense putting things off for later.

Mrs. Young's car wasn't in the yard when I came chasing down the drive to the maternity home, and I took that as a good sign. I wasn't looking to come up with some half-baked excuse to explain my presence to her. I was never any good at fibbing, or maybe it was just that Ma had an innate talent for detecting untruths. Hurrying along, I stopped on the back step to catch my breath. From inside the kitchen came a jumble of voices and rattling dishes as I opened the door.

"Hi Tulia," chimed Claire when I walked in. She'd helped out one day in the laundry room when I was there with Ma. I knew some of the mothers stayed on after their babies were born to pay off whatever they owed. Ma used to say it was decent of Mrs. Young, since *most of them show up without a dime in their pocket but Mrs. Young never turns them away*—Ma's words, not mine.

I walked right on through like I had every business in the world being there, saying a quick hello to Claire as I breezed past. I'd most likely find Becky in the nursery looking after the babies. A feeling of relief warmed me inside. I'd get down to the bottom of it once and for all. Most surely, Finny had been mistaken about the girl he saw. This would soon be straightened away.

I'd been to the nursery a few times in the past to see the babies and knew my way. With Ma stuck down in the laundry, she didn't always know my whereabouts when she went to hang out diapers. I couldn't help sneaking a peek at those precious little babies from time to time.

The walls of the nursery expanded beneath the sound of crying babies when I walked in. Some of the girls were trying to quiet them down, but there were far more babies than what there was help for. Hurrying toward one of the cribs, I picked up a crying baby that had been at the home for several months waiting to be adopted. I called her Marie, after one of the quints. I always felt bad for those ones, waiting for a family and a proper name. Some babies were gone almost before they arrived, especially when some rich couple put in a special request like they were ordering from a catalogue. When that phone call came from Mrs. Young they'd hurry off to adopt the baby with no time to spare. But what about the babies people weren't so anxious to adopt? Those were the ones I felt sorry for. Babies might not all be born perfect, but they shouldn't be punished because of it.

A girl I'd never seen before was changing one of the baby's diapers. "Where's Becky?" I asked over the wailing that was filling the room.

"I don't know any Beckys," she said. Resting a baby against her oversized belly, she swayed back and forth to try and quiet it.

"She just started working here a few weeks back. She's got blonde hair. She's real pretty. She's got blue eyes," I said, jiggling Marie the way I'd seen my sister Linda do while resting a little one on each hip.

"I've been here a month. I don't know any Becky," said the girl, making some shushing sounds. But then Becky walked into the nursery with an armload of bottles and I hurried toward her, relieved. I took a bottle for Marie, who was now screaming blue murder.

"Why didn't Ma tell me you were here?" I asked, shoving the bottle into Marie's wailing mouth. Her lips puckered around the rubber nipple.

"Does Ma know where you are?" Becky demanded, looking not the least bit happy to see me. "You'd better go home, Tulia, before there's trouble."

"I don't need Ma to run my life." I was old enough to make some decisions for myself. If I couldn't take care of myself at twelve, there was no help for me. Turning from Becky, I laid Marie back down in her crib with her bottle. It was hard to have a conversation with a baby in your arms.

"Debbie...Debbie. Leave those bottles. I need you to help the new girl get settled in. Don't just stand there, move along." Mrs. Young's voice cut through me and I spun around. She wouldn't want me in the nursery, let alone making anything of the babies—I was sure of it.

"Does your mother know you're here?" Mrs. Young

said stiffly when she saw me standing there. I shook my head as the reality of the situation dawned on me. I stood staring at Becky. The look on her face said it all. Mrs. Young barked out my name and I jumped. I looked from Mrs. Young to Becky, waiting for an explanation that was no longer necessary.

# Chapter Seven

On my way back home, I struggled to hold in the tears. My chest ached and I gulped in air. If it wasn't for the fact that I dare not stay away too long, I would have sat down by the roadside and bawled my eyes out.

*Debbie*—Mrs. Young had called her Debbie. There was no mistaking it.

It all made sense to me then; the big fight Ma and Becky had, Becky's sudden disappearance, Ma's unwillingness to tell me what was going on. It all made such perfect, horrible sense. Why had I refused to believe Finny? My feet shuffled clumsily down the dirt road toward home as I fought to come up with the right words to make Ma come clean. I was tired of being lied to.

The Merrys were standing in the entryway with their jackets on when I came charging in through the doorway. Ma gave me a dark look as I boldly walked in past her. She'd be livid that I'd left the house without telling her first, but I didn't care. She wouldn't make a scene in front of company.

"So nice seeing you this evening, Tulia," said Mrs. Merry, flashing me a cheery grin. I offered a quick counterfeit smile and hung up my jacket.

"We'll stay in touch, Naomi," added Mrs. Merry, squeezing Ma's hands a little too hard before leaving. They were all in on it together—Ma, Mrs. Young, and the Merrys. I was sure of it. Ma wasn't fooling me in the least.

I waited in the hallway, impatiently tapping my foot as I waited for the Merrys to leave. I was ready to get some answers.

"Tulia May," Ma said, squeezing the words out as soon as she'd sent the Merrys on their way, "I have half a mind to ground you for the next six months. Where have you been off to without permission this time of the evening?"

I pulled in a big breath. I needed to take time to collect my thoughts as I decided how best to begin. I guess Ma took that to mean that I wasn't going to answer, because her voice came out strong and steady when she said, "Tulia May, I asked you a question—now, where were you?" That's when I let loose.

"Where was I, Ma? You want to know where I was? I'll tell you where I was. I was at the maternity home." The words came out of me fast and furious and without an ounce of respect. I could feel my face was flushed.

"The maternity home?" The surprised look on her face gave me satisfaction for a brief moment. How dare she keep all this a secret from me?

"Yeah, Ma, that's right, the *Ideal* Maternity Home. Only it's not so ideal, as we both know...and guess who I saw there, Ma? Just take a guess." Ma didn't look like someone who was about to own up to anything. "I saw, Debbie, Ma—Debbie."

She faltered. "I...I don't know who you mean, Debbie."

"Sure you do, Ma. Only you know what? It wasn't Debbie at all. It was really Becky—our Becky. Imagine finding out my own sister is one of Mrs. Young's wayward girls. You know, Ma, the girls you always wanted me to stay away from in case what they had would rub off on me one day."

By that time I was trembling. Mrs. Young gave the girls new names when they came to the home—to protect their privacy. I knew that for a fact, because Ma told me one time. She went to speak, but I wasn't through. "Did you really think you could fool me? That I'd never find out? The maternity home's just up the road from us. You always treat me like a little kid, like I don't know anything."

Ma looked away, stubborn to the core. "Tulia," she said quietly, but I had no desire to hear what she was about to say.

"And the Merrys? I know they're involved. Mrs. Featherstone said just a few weeks ago that they wanted to adopt one of the babies at the home."

She sighed with impatience, because, really, *the jig was up*—Finny Paul's words, not mine.

"They're to adopt Becky's child, if you must know—if it's a boy," she added.

That immediately put me on the defensive. I was filled with questions that needed answers. "You mean they only want Becky's baby if it's a boy? Bad enough they can't have their own baby, but what gives them the right to be so picky? A baby is a baby is a baby."

"Tulia, you have no right to judge. The Merrys are set on having a boy. One way or another they'll get one. At least with them we'll know where the child is going."

*No right to judge*—strange words coming from Ma.

"And if it's *not* a boy?" I asked. It was a fair question to ask. Too much seemed to be riding on the chance that Becky would have a boy.

Ma looked away again.

"If it's not a boy?" I repeated, louder this time. She looked at me with hollow eyes and for a moment I saw the toll this was taking on her. The happy face she'd put on for the Merrys was just an act.

"Mrs. Young will find a good home for the child. She has a list of prospective parents—rich people from the States."

"What's wrong with the Merrys adopting a girl?" I stated.

"They don't want a girl."

"Tell them they have to take what they get or else have

their own baby. That's what everyone else does. They don't get to pick and choose, so why should the Merrys?"

"The Merrys are farmers, Tulia. They want a boy—to help out on the farm."

"A girl can do the same thing, Ma. You know that and I know that." Of all the pathetic excuses.

"If the baby's a girl, she will be well taken care of with a world of advantages the rest of us can only dream about. Now, we've discussed this enough, Tulia. Mrs. Young is being most generous in this situation your sister has found herself in."

"Listen at you, Ma...this is all wrong. You can't just give Becky's baby away to strangers. It's your grandchild and my niece or nephew." Maybe if I found the right words, Ma would change her mind.

"It's what Becky wants, Tulia. As much as you'd like to think otherwise, this isn't your decision to make. It's Becky's, and Becky has decided to give her baby up for adoption. Now, if the Merrys end up adopting the baby—"

I rolled my eyes. "You mean, if the baby's a boy."

"If it's a boy," Ma said, nodding in agreement. "Then we may see the child from time to time, but of course, he won't be told who we are."

"And if it's a girl?" Tears sprung to my eyes and I wiped them way. This seemed so unfair. "Then what, Ma? We'll never see her—that's what."

"I'm sorry, Tulia, but that's the way it's going to be."

An idea struck me just then. "Why can't *we* look after the baby?"

"We most certainly cannot. I've had my share of raising babies over the years. You have no idea what you're saying, Tulia, no idea at all." The loose skin around her jaw wobbled as she spoke. She was flabbergasted that I would even suggest such a thing, but I knew what her real concern was.

"You're just worried about what other people will think, that's all," I stated, stamping the words into place.

"Berate me all you want, Tulia, but believe it or not, I'm protecting your sister's reputation. Mrs. Young is discreet. Do you know what would happen if this got out? Becky's life would be ruined—that's what."

"You mean *your* life, don't you, Ma?" At that point I'd had enough. I started up the stairs to my room.

"You keep this to yourself, now, Tulia. You hear me? If this gets out you'll be the one responsible for ruining your sister's life," she said as I clomped up the stairs.

Slamming my door, I flopped down onto the bed.

"You stay away from that maternity home, Tulia," Ma said, her muffled warning penetrating my bedroom door. "Do you hear me? You're not to go out there. You leave Becky alone. If you don't, I'll send her off to a home in Halifax."

I reached for my scrapbook and pulled it down onto the bed with me. Mrs. Dionne had five babies all at once and I bet she didn't consider adopting any of them out. Ma said the adoption was Becky's idea, but was that the truth? It was clear that Ma wasn't above lying when it suited her. I wasn't about to accept whatever was told me as law, not like I once did. Her only concern was keeping the neighbours from talking. I knew how judgemental people could be. I'd heard plenty of talk over the years from some of the old biddies in the community. They looked down their noses at Mrs. Young's girls. While Ma never voiced an opinion publicly, I knew she shared their opinion of the girls who came to the home. You'd have thought over time people would have become used to the maternity home being in their backyard. Now Becky was one of those girls. Ma would never live it down if that got out.

Determination took hold of me that night as I lay there looking at my scrapbook. Ma could take her high-and-mighty attitude and toss it into the cove. One way or another, I was going to let Becky know that family sticks together. Becky's baby was family and you don't give away family. Together we'd figure out a way for her to keep the baby. While Ma might have thought she could keep me away from Becky, I promised myself that I'd find a way to let my sister know she didn't have to go through this alone.

The next morning, I ate in silence while Ma got ready to go off to the maternity home. "Magnolia's coming in on the train the day after tomorrow...alone," she said tersely, as she buttoned her sweater. Normally I'd have squealed with delight over the news. Aunt Maggie was so much fun to be around.

"Art couldn't come this time," she continued as if answering my unspoken question. Uncle Art usually drove Aunt Maggie down. He'd stay for about a week and then drive back home, leaving Aunt Maggie to return later on the train. I stopped eating for a second, stubbornly refusing to acknowledge what Ma had just told me.

"Look, Tulia, you can snub me all you want, but it's just childish behaviour on your part." She cleared her throat. "You might think I'm being cruel to your sister, but I'm her mother. I know what's best—not you." I could sense her standing in the doorway but I pretended not to.

"Make sure the spare room is presentable," she said before the door closed behind her.

And then a thought came to me like a shot from Finny's .22. I knew then who could adopt Becky's baby. It was the perfect solution. Why hadn't I thought of it before?

# Chapter Eight

꧁꧂

All the frustration I was feeling with Ma went into scrubbing the floor of the spare bedroom. While I worked I contemplated the situation with Becky. The excitement I usually felt with Aunt Maggie's visit was overshadowed by my fear that Ma might find a way to ruin any plan I came up with to keep Becky's baby in the family. I was determined to do what I had to. It wouldn't do to have Becky's baby adopted out to strangers. The Merrys seemed like nice people, but they weren't family. I couldn't imagine never telling him I was his aunt or that Ma was his grandma. Worse yet, if it was a girl we'd never know what happened to her. There just had to be a better way.

My arms ached from scrubbing, but I ignored it as I bore down harder on the floorboards. Why was Ma being so difficult? Why didn't she want to hold Becky's baby and play peek-a-boo the way she did with her other grandbabies? The more I scrubbed at the bedroom floor that morning, the more I became determined to make my plan work. Aunt Maggie and Uncle Art would make the perfect parents for Becky's little baby.

I'd speak to Becky first. Becky was the baby's mother. It would only be fair. Getting her to agree wouldn't be a problem. I knew she'd be so happy to have Aunt Maggie adopt her baby. I was surprised she hadn't thought of it herself. Or maybe that was Ma's fault. No one else in the family would have to know. It could be our secret, Becky and Ma, Aunt Maggie, Uncle Art, and me. I was good at keeping secrets. No one found out how Harry Lawson's milking cow mysteriously ended up in old Mrs. Story's front yard one morning in June. It was warm and I had my bedroom window open that night. The soft clanging of a cowbell is what woke me. When I looked out into the moonlight, I saw two people leading a cow down the road. I sat beside the open window and listened to them talking. I knew who the voices belonged to. For weeks folks speculated as to who could have pulled off such a prank.

As I dumped the dirty scrub water out behind the house, I thought my way through what needed to be done next. I wouldn't dare risk going to the maternity home to see Becky. If Mrs. Young caught me in there again she'd most surely tell Ma. I'd been given strict orders to stay away, and Ma wasn't one to make idle threats. She'd send

Becky off to a church-run home in Halifax, I was sure of it. I'd have to meet Becky outside someplace where we wouldn't be seen. It wasn't as if the girls weren't allowed outside. It was always busy at the home with so many girls coming in and out. No one would even see her slip away.

I'd ask for Finny Paul's help. There was no way around that. He was the only one I could trust to get a note to Becky, no questions asked—and I knew Finny wouldn't ask any questions. I wasn't ready to tell him about Becky's predicament even though I knew he already suspected. For sure he'd eventually find out, as much time as he spent spying out there. But Finny wasn't one to judge. I guess being judged yourself makes you more considerate that way.

By mid-morning the spare room was presentable for company. I'd even put a bouquet of wildflowers on the dresser. Aunt Maggie was especially fond of daisies and there were plenty growing behind the house. There was still an hour or two before Ma would be home from the maternity home. I'd have time to get out to the cove and back.

"I've got an important mission for you," I said to Finny as he cast his line into the water. He turned, smiling. Finny was always one to be counted on and never one to turn down an important mission.

"Consider it done," he said when I handed him the envelope with the name *Debbie* written on it. If he thought my request was an odd one, he didn't let on.

I left the cove that morning trusting that Finny would come through for me. For the time being, I'd act as though everything was fine. Aunt Maggie was arriving tomorrow. Things would soon be better.

Aunt Maggie stepped off the train wearing a burgundy jacket and matching skirt that flapped in the wind. The little bit of lip rouge she was wearing gave her a fresh look. She looked quite smart by East Chester standards; she always did. The sight of her reminded me of the air-dried laundry Ma used to bring in off the clothesline when I was small. Sometimes I would dive beneath the clothes when she dumped them on the bed to be folded. They were warm from being out in the sun all day. They smelled of sunshine and fresh ocean air and I'd cocoon myself inside them.

"Get out from there, Tulia May," Ma would say, and she'd pull me out from beneath the clothes. I'd grab hold of one of her skirts and race through the house, dragging it behind me. She'd send Becky to chase after me. Becky would catch me and throw me onto the bed. We'd all three be laughing. Aunt Maggie still smelled like that fresh sun-dried laundry on Ma's bed when I hugged her at the station.

"Your hemline's a disgrace, Magnolia. Why, your knees

are nearly sticking out," Ma said as Aunt Maggie wrapped her arms around her. "I dare say Art should make sure you're properly dressed before you step outside the door." She sounded harsh but I could tell she was pleased to see her sister. She always was.

"Fashions change, Naomi," Aunt Maggie said as she breezed into the passenger's side of the car, "and so do hemlines." She flashed me a smile over her shoulder.

Not only was Aunt Maggie my favourite person of all time, she knew about the latest hairstyles and fashions. She kept up to date with what all the actors and actresses in Hollywood were doing. She also knew all the names of the popular songs on the radio and the words to go with them. Aunt Maggie was everything that Ma wasn't, right filled with modern ideas. Ma would tell Aunt Maggie that Ontario living was making her too big for her britches. She would also say that not having kids made people selfish. Aunt Maggie would just laugh at Ma. It was such a ridiculous thing to say; I don't even think Ma believed her own words. Aunt Maggie and Uncle Art weren't one bit selfish; they were far from it. They were generous and loving and happier than I ever thought two people could be. And that's why I knew they'd agree to take Becky's baby. Everyone in the family said it was a darn shame they hadn't been blessed with any children of their own.

Ma and Aunt Maggie jabbered all the way home. The sun streamed in through the car window and I felt the warmth of happiness filling my heart. From the back seat I imagined Aunt Maggie holding a baby in her arms, looking happier than I'd ever seen. I saw the baby dressed up in a gown that Ma had sewn herself. I smiled. I wanted it so badly I was almost bursting with hope. It was an easy thing to believe. What if this whole predicament of Becky's turned out to be a blessing in disguise?

# Chapter Nine

Ma took the next week off work, the same way she did every year when Aunt Maggie came to visit. She was good at stretching her pennies and always put a bit aside for those times when company came to stay.

"It wouldn't be much of a visit for you if I worked the whole time you were here," Ma said one time when Aunt Maggie mentioned that her visit was costing Ma money. She even offered to make up the difference.

"A hotel would cost," Aunt Maggie said.

"This isn't a hotel, Magnolia, and don't you worry. We'll be just fine. That's why I take in the sewing—for those little extras that pop up." Aunt Maggie never brought the subject up again.

On Aunt Maggie's first evening home she brought out a silver locket and gave it to me. "I picked it up in Toronto a few months back and thought of you." The locket was in the shape of a small heart. I knew immediately what pictures I could put in it. I hugged Aunt Maggie and ran off to my room. I went through the magazines she'd brought with her, searching for a picture of the quints that would fit. I finally located a small likeness of them in an advertisement for a commemorative plate. Carefully cutting around the image, I was able to make it small enough to fit inside the locket. Since each quint was so tiny, I then clipped out a larger photo of one of them to put on the other side. After all, they *were* identical. I was sure it was the best gift Aunt Maggie had ever given me. I lay in bed that night feeling the comfort of the tiny locket against my skin. Everything was going to be fine once I told Becky my plan. Aunt Maggie and Uncle Art would adopt Becky's baby. I was sure of it.

—

I couldn't say what it was, but something felt different about Aunt Maggie's visit this time around. I wondered if it had to do with what was going on with Becky—all the secrecy involved. It didn't help that I was keeping things from Aunt Maggie, but until I could talk to Becky it was necessary. Also there was Aunt Maggie, who seemed preoccupied with what was going on in Europe.

"Do you think there'll be a war?" I overheard her ask Ma in the sewing room that first night after she arrived. She was speaking low and I figured she didn't want me to hear. I was down the hall in my room going through the new batch of magazines she had brought with her from Ontario, and Ma was showing off the dress she was making for Mrs. Walker to wear on her trip to Boston later this summer.

"With what's going on overseas, I wouldn't be surprised," said Ma seconds before the sewing machine started up. Quickly snapping off the light, I settled into bed and pulled the quilt up over me. Their words joggled through me and I shook off the strange sensation that was stepping along my spine. I didn't know that Ma even cared about what was going on in Europe, let alone had an opinion about it. We'd never discussed the subject. I'd sometimes hear her make a comment or two about it when we were in town, but that was about it. Being as busy as what she was at the maternity home, I thought she wasn't interested or else had little concern over it. Finny, on the other hand, knew plenty when it came to the subject of war. Mr. Jefferson used to give him his old newspapers and he'd read up on all the world events. He found it all a little *too* fascinating for my liking. Maybe his father being a war vet played a part in that. I think Finny secretly wished to be a hero like his Pa.

"I'll join up if there's another war," he said one day.

"Oh, Finny Paul, you're too young to be in the army. Besides, there's not going to be a war," I'd answered back. As I listened to Ma and Aunt Maggie in the sewing room that night, I wasn't so sure. Ma was by no means an optimist, and looking on the dark side of things seemed to suit her, but hearing her admit that war was a possibility filled me with worry.

I lay awake for what seemed like hours. I could hear Ma and Aunt Maggie talking long into the night. If they were discussing a war, I didn't want to hear. Instead, I pushed my thoughts in a happier direction. Both the *Standard* and *Star Weekly* magazines Aunt Maggie brought with her had plenty of quint photos in them. The *Standard* magazines were filled with photos of the King and Queen's visit to Canada this past May. I especially liked the photo of the quintuplets all dressed up to meet the royal couple. They were each wearing a long dress with lacy ruffles, matching bonnets, and tiny white gloves. I thought it was quite possibly the sweetest picture I'd seen of the quints to date, and I fell asleep wishing I would one day visit them in Quintland.

"Lord knows the world isn't as safe as it once was. Sanctions. Countries under occupation. This Adolf Hitler is a danger to us all," Ma said, setting the table the next evening at suppertime. It was the first time Hitler's name had been mentioned in our house. Were things in the world really that bad?

"Art's planning to enlist," Aunt Maggie suddenly

blurted out during supper. She was doing a good job of holding back the tears as she took a bite of roast beef, but I could tell she was upset. Her words jolted me. Ma seemed surprised at the news, although her tone suggested otherwise when she said, "I did wonder." She casually reached for the water pitcher.

"But he's a lawyer," I quickly spoke up.

"War doesn't care who you are or what you do for a living," said Ma, filling our tumblers. A long stretch of silence followed and Aunt Maggie made a strange sound. I looked over at her. Her bottom lip was trembling slightly as she stabbed at the food on her plate.

"I've been invited to go swimming the day after tomorrow," I said, quickly changing the subject, not only for Aunt Maggie's benefit but for my own as well. I didn't want to hear about the possibility of a war and I certainly didn't want to talk about Uncle Art maybe joining up if there was one. It hadn't been that long ago since the last war. Two of my brothers had signed up back then, and Ma's brother, Oscar. That was all before I was even born. According to Aunt Maggie, every night they were gone Ma lit a candle for their safe return. I never did get to meet my Uncle Oscar. Aunt Maggie said he was handsome and funny and wanted to help save the world.

"So idealistic," she said with a sad smile. Too bad handsome and funny isn't enough to keep you alive during war. Why couldn't this Hitler person leave everyone alone?

"You most certainly cannot go gallivanting around while we have company." Ma didn't even wait to hear any of the details. "Besides, it's not proper for young girls to be running about wild through the community."

"Oh Ma, we're not a pack of dogs." To my left I heard a small snort. Out of the corner of my eye I could see Aunt Maggie smiling. I was glad.

"It's just Hope and Marlee, and they're going to Stoddard's Pond. And I never get invited anywhere." I tried not to sound too desperate. Ma wasn't one to buckle in to whining and moaning. My real plan, the one I couldn't tell Ma about, was to go out to the maternity home and speak with Becky. If Finny had delivered my note, she'd be expecting me. Somehow I had to convince Ma to let me go.

"People get ideas, Tulia, and none of them good," Ma said, dipping into the butter with a knife. If she didn't give in I'd have to come up with some other excuse, and I wasn't one for inventing fancy stories. I looked over at Aunt Maggie for some help, hoping she'd step in and take my side as she had a number of times in the past when Ma was being unreasonable. She cleared her throat before speaking up.

"It may not be my place to say anything, but you can't shield Tulia forever, Naomi." Ma rolled her eyes in Aunt Maggie's direction as she buttered a slice of bread. "Stoddard's isn't that far away. I used to go when I was

Tulia's age. I'm sure you did too."

"You should stay out of things that don't concern you, Magnolia," Mama snapped back. "I'd hardly call looking out for Tulia's best interests shielding her. Now, can we eat our meal in peace?" Aunt Maggie looked at me and shrugged as if to say she'd tried her best. It looked as though I'd have to find some other excuse to slip off and meet with Becky. The problem was, I wasn't sure I was devious enough for that. It wasn't as if good ideas fell down like rain for me. Ma usually had a way of sensing when I was up to something. I could only hope her guard was down a bit with Aunt Maggie here to distract her.

That night Ma stuck her head inside my bedroom just before bedtime and whispered my name. It reminded me of the times when I was small and she'd come into my room to hear my prayers. I rose up on my elbows, wondering what she wanted. For a moment she said nothing as if searching for something to say.

"You may go swimming with the girls...for an hour," she said quietly.

"Thanks, Ma." It seemed strange, her giving in like that. While I wasn't about to question her change of heart, I knew Aunt Maggie had something to do with it.

"And Tulia?" she added before closing the door.

"Yes, Ma?" I was about ready to jump through the ceiling with glee, but I couldn't let her know. Cool and calm always worked best with Ma.

"I want you straight home afterwards. Do you hear? I trust you'll stay out of trouble," she added, then closed the door. I breathed in my pleasure from beneath the quilt. Aunt Maggie sure had a way with Ma that the rest of us didn't.

# Chapter Ten

Because of the secret I was holding in my heart, I found it difficult to enjoy Aunt Maggie's visit. We did all the things Aunt Maggie enjoyed doing whenever she came home, yet it was hard to think of anything other than my upcoming meeting with Becky. Whenever Aunt Maggie was visiting East Chester, she came down the stairs each morning wearing a pair of dungarees. Immediately after breakfast she'd head out to do some gardening, something she said she missed most about living here. Ma wasn't usually far behind. By mid-morning we'd stop for a break and sit under the maple trees and sip lemonade. Ma seemed more relaxed when Aunt Maggie was home and was even kind of fun to be around. Those were the times when she wasn't near as bossy and often laughed at Aunt Maggie's stories.

Ma drove us to Chester Basin the next afternoon and we had a picnic down by the water. Aunt Maggie fed the gulls while Ma admonished her for doing so.

"The dirty, wretched things," she said, watching one fly off with a crust of her homemade bread in its beak. She then warned that one of those "wretched things" followed Jordan Russell home one time and did its business all over his front yard. Ma didn't appreciate it much when her story made us both laugh.

My upcoming meeting with Becky played steadily on my mind. While I was sure she'd be thrilled when I told her about my plan to have Uncle Art and Aunt Maggie adopt her baby, I wouldn't breathe easy until we reached an agreement. With everything me and Becky had shared over the years, it made no sense for me to feel so anxious. Ma would be livid that I'd gone behind her back, but that was to be expected. Some things are more important than a few hurt feelings. Ma would just have to get over it, and I was certain she would in time. *Some things you do for the greater good*—Mrs. Jefferson's words, not mine. Of course, Aunt Maggie would step in to defend me; that much I could count on. After all, she'd be the one getting a baby to love. While Ma would never come right out and admit that she respected her younger sister, she always told people that Aunt Maggie was very level-headed. If anyone could convince Ma that Aunt Maggie and Uncle Art adopting Becky's baby was the perfect solution for everyone, it was Aunt Maggie.

To folks driving through East Chester on any given day of the week, that big old maternity home likely seemed out of place standing in the middle of nowhere like that. It put me in mind of what a hotel would look like if ever I'd seen one, which I hadn't. It didn't start out that big but grew over time as more and more girls found themselves *in the family way*—Ma's words, not mine. Long before Ma started working there I would wonder what it looked like inside. Some of the kids at school used to say it was haunted, they even claimed that a ghost walked the grounds on foggy nights, but I saw or heard no evidence of that whenever I went to help Ma with the laundry.

Mrs. James, the postmistress, used to say that the Youngs coming out to East Chester like that and setting up business was to keep people from knowing what was really going on.

"They're selling those babies and making a bundle doing it." Mrs. James was adamant about that. I asked her how much a baby would be worth. "More than any of us regular folks can afford," she said.

When I came home and repeated what Mrs. James had said I was told in no uncertain terms that Mrs. James was better at stirring the pot than she was sorting the mail and that I should know better than to repeat the tongue-waggings of narrow-minded people.

"These girls deserve their privacy and Lila should be commended, not condemned," Ma added.

I hid in the shadows of the chicken coop looking out toward the maternity home that late August day. I could only imagine that Ma was more than grateful for Mrs. Young's privacy policy now that she'd sent her own daughter there.

The same seed of doubt that had followed me out to the maternity home began to sprout into a nagging fear as I waited for Becky. Tucked safely behind the Youngs' chicken coop, I had a clear view of the back door. Two times I jumped as the door opened, only to be disappointed. What if Finny hadn't been able to get my note to Becky? Moreover, what if Ma had warned her to stay away from me and she wasn't planning to show? So many things ran through my mind. In my note, I'd said for her to meet me at one. Mrs. Young made the girls chip in with the chores. What if Becky was scheduled to do something at one o'clock? As time went by and there was still no sign of her, I started to panic. I only had an hour before Ma would send a search party out for me, meaning Aunt Maggie. This was my only chance to keep Becky's baby out of the hands of strangers.

But then my heart fluttered when Becky stepped out onto the doorstep. She pulled her sweater around herself and looked casually about the backyard, as if enjoying the scenery. I was surprised to see the bump beneath the light blue duster she was wearing. All those baggy dresses she'd worn when she was home last. Why hadn't

I figured it out for myself?

I peeked out around the corner of the building as she began to stroll across the grass in my direction. When she stuck her head around the chicken coop, I threw my arms around her neck.

"Does Ma know you're here?" she said, abruptly pulling away from me.

"She thinks I'm down at Stoddard's Pond."

Without hesitation I went on to tell her my reason for being there, and that Aunt Maggie and Uncle Art would make perfect parents. And as I waited for her to express her undying gratitude to me for coming up with such a wonderful plan, I could tell something wasn't right. She was shaking her head. When she said, "I don't want the family knowing, I don't want anyone to know, Tulia," my heart sank.

"But it's just Aunt Maggie. She won't tell anyone. She can say she got the baby from an adoption agency in Ontario. No one will suspect a thing," I quickly added. Why was Becky being so difficult? Did she really think Aunt Maggie wouldn't keep her secret?

Just then another idea came to me.

"Why don't you and William get married?" I said, taking her hands in mine. It seemed the most obvious solution now that I thought of it. I remembered how happy she'd been at Christmas when she told me about him. But she pulled her hands from mine and turned her back on me.

"He's married, Tulia," she whispered, so softly I wasn't sure what she'd said until she repeated it. "I found out he was married. I...I thought...." She was close to tears, but then suddenly got hold of herself. She turned to face me again wearing a look of determination. I knew that side of Becky, the side that kicked in when things got rough.

"The baby will go to a good home. Mrs. Young is making sure of it." But I wasn't fooled by what she said. They were Ma's words, not Becky's.

"It's Ma, isn't it? Ma's the one making you do this."

"No, Tulia." She was shaking her head, but it wasn't too late to change her mind. Ma had no business telling Becky what to do with her own baby.

"You don't have do what Ma wants, Becky. She's not the boss; you are."

"A lot you know. Ma wanted Aunt Maggie to take the baby, but I don't want that. Why is it so hard for you to believe?" *Because I know you wouldn't give your baby away to strangers unless Ma was making you,* I wanted to say.

"But Becky...family sticks together. Remember?

"Look, Tulia, you're only twelve. Life isn't as simple as what you think and this isn't your first day at school. Now go home and forget this silly idea of yours. Nothing you say will make me change my mind."

As Becky hurried toward the home, a lump in my throat restricted my breathing. I would never in a million years have thought Becky could be so cruel.

By the time I made it back home, I'd managed to pull myself together. The only thing I could hope for now was that Becky would have a boy and the Merrys would adopt him. We'd at least get to see him from time to time. Coming to that realization, I was sure it was how Ma felt about it as well. It was more than likely the cause for all their arguments. If Ma was stubborn and unbending, Becky was even more so. It was easier to blame Ma for giving Becky's baby away than to think it was really Becky's idea.

Opening the front door, I momentarily stopped in the hallway. Noting the absence of sound coming from Ma's sewing room, I took it as a good sign. Meant Ma wasn't purposely waiting to confront me about my afternoon at Stoddard's Pond. I crept up the stairs, glad that she was nowhere in sight. She was most likely out digging in the garden. With Aunt Maggie's help, there wasn't a weed to be seen and the garden was swarming with small green cucumbers peeking out from underneath the leaves. Things seemed to be going in my favour until Aunt Maggie appeared in the upstairs hallway.

I pulled in a quick gasp. "Aunt Maggie, you scared me," I blurted out, my heart beating like a drum inside my chest.

"For someone who just spent an hour swimming, you look awfully dry," she remarked. There was an odd expression on her face. I felt like the cat that got caught swallowing the canary.

"There were things I had to do, Aunt Maggie. Ma never lets me.... Where is Ma?" I was about to get busted and would probably end up grounded for the rest of my natural- born days and there was nothing I could say in my own defence. I thought about it later. I shouldn't have gone off to see Becky. I thought this would all be so easy to fix. I had the perfect solution, so I thought.

"She's in the garden," said Aunt Maggie.

"Please don't tell," I pleaded.

"I remember what it is to be young, Tulia," she said. "Sometimes a girl has things to do."

Hugging Aunt Maggie, I hurried off to my room to change. Ma would notice if I had on the same clothes I'd left home in. Reaching the doorway, I turned back toward Aunt Maggie. She was smiling. I couldn't help thinking what a wonderful mother she would have been.

## Chapter Eleven

❦

On the last day of Aunt Maggie's visit, we drove out to Fox Point to see the aunties. There were two of them, well into their eighties by that time, and still living in the house that had been built by our ancestors in the 1800s. I never visited my grandparents who lived nearby as they had both died long before I was born, but I have vivid memories of visiting the aunties faithfully every year.

Back when Becky lived at home she was always Auntie May's favourite, even though I was the one who shared her name. Auntie May would tell Becky to help herself to an extra molasses cookie as Becky gingerly reached into the jar being held before her. I never minded being slighted in that way, as Auntie May's cookies were as hard as flint. So you can imagine my surprise that day when we drove out to visit and Auntie May's voice rang out, "How's my favourite girl?" I reasoned she must be talking to Aunt Maggie, most certainly not me. I stood, momentarily stunned by her outburst, then stumbled in through the doorway thanks to a small push on the back of the head from Ma. I ended up practically falling into Auntie May's waiting arms. She grabbed fast to me, rocking back and forth. Wrapped up tight in Auntie May's bosom, I struggled for breath.

"Oh, Tulia May," she continued before releasing me. "Look at you, all grown up." I was surprised by her show of affection. When in the world had I become her favourite girl? She then let out a squeal when she saw Aunt Maggie.

"Come, Vi," she cried, pulling Aunt Maggie into an embrace. "We've got company. It's Naomi and Tulia—and look who they brought with them."

"Hold on, May." Auntie Vi came out from the kitchen, wiping her hands on her apron. She was wearing a big smile. "Let's see who we have here."

Auntie Vi looped her arm into Aunt Maggie's and all but dragged her into the parlour. Ma and me followed like obedient children and sat down when we were instructed to. Tea was served along with an ample supply of Auntie May's molasses cookies. The conversation went along smoothly until Auntie Vi brought up the subject of Mrs. Young and the maternity home.

"I presume you're still working out at the Youngs', Naomi," said Auntie May well into our visit. She looked at Ma as if daring her to engage in conversation about the maternity home. The mention of the Youngs jolted me a bit. Could the aunties possibly know about Becky? But I quickly reasoned that wasn't possible. Although by the looks on both of their faces, they had heard some bit of juicy gossip and were dying to tell.

"I'm still working in the laundry. I assume that's what you mean." Ma pressed her hands together on her lap.

"We followed the trial," said Auntie Vi, delicately taking a sip of tea. "It caused quite the buzz. Did you read up on it, Naomi?" Auntie Vi was treading on thin ice.

"Trial?" Aunt Maggie seemed shocked.

"Manslaughter," said Auntie Vi, pursing her lips and nodding at Aunt Maggie.

"Manslaughter? Naomi, you never—"

"I don't know all the details and it really isn't my place to know. I just work there," said Ma.

"Yes, but Naomi, there must have been something...I mean, people aren't charged for no good reason."

"You know very well how things get exaggerated, Magnolia. Besides, that was months ago." Ma's words came out stiff and unnatural, although I'm not sure anyone else noticed.

"With all the evidence against them, it surprised us when they got off scot-free," said Auntie May. She looked at Auntie Vi and they both nodded. Ma shifted uncomfortably. I'd never heard her say a word against the Youngs and I knew she wasn't about to start anytime soon. With Ma, Mrs. Young came first.

Aunt Maggie insisted on hearing the details and the aunties willingly obliged.

"They say the poor girl went into shock and Lila didn't have a clue what to do. Couldn't do a thing to save her," said Auntie Vi, letting out a big sigh.

"How horrible for that young girl and her family," said Aunt Maggie.

"Tragedy brings everyone looking to lay blame, and believe me, they all have an opinion, whether they know the facts or not," said Ma.

"I heard there's been a call to close them down," said Auntie Vi.

"The Youngs have a lucrative business going and during these times that means something...for everyone in East Chester, not just me. I would assume there could be some who are jealous over the Youngs' success. What many don't know is that there are inspections and they've passed each and every one." I did know about the inspections. Mrs. Young usually expected a supply of new diapers and gowns to be sewn. Ma would sometimes stay up half the night working on them.

"I daresay that young girl's family doesn't care about inspections or how much money the Youngs are bringing into the community," said Auntie Vi with a grunt.

"Women have died in childbirth from the beginning of time. That's a well-known fact," said Ma. I could see her struggling to remain composed. But when Auntie

May said, "Some would wonder if she's even qualified to deliver babies," that did it.

"Say what you will, but Lila gives these girls a new start. She takes them in when no one else will. She—" Ma stopped abruptly. I glanced over at Aunt Maggie. Ma was speaking altogether too ardently. The look on Aunt Maggie's face told me she could see it too. I reached for a cookie but knocked a spoon onto the floor. I'd never heard Ma speak this way about the Youngs or the maternity home or anything before.

"I didn't know you felt so strongly," said Aunt Maggie. A strange look befell Ma's face, as if she'd only just realized she shouldn't have gotten so carried away.

"Mrs. Young has been good to me. I have to take people the way I find them," she added.

We were all unusually quiet on the ride home as we privately digested our visit with the aunties. Thinking about what all the aunties had to say about the maternity home, I couldn't help wondering about Becky. Was it safe for her to be there? I was sure Ma would tell me there was nothing to worry about, and I wanted to believe that, really I did.

As we came upon the Fox Point Cemetery there was a car parked alongside the road. I recognized it right away. Ma drove on, staring straight at the road ahead. I looked in at the cemetery as we passed by. Mr. and Mrs. Young were walking across the green turf, past the rows of tombstones. A hard lump formed in my throat when I saw what Mr. Young was carrying under his arm. I'd seen some stacked up in the back of Firmin Jefferson's store one time when Mrs. Jefferson sent me to bring out a pail of salt herring. It was a wooden butterbox.

I knew then that another baby had died.

—

The sun was setting orange when the passenger train came into the station. Aunt Maggie was wearing the same snazzy outfit she'd worn the day she arrived. I wished her visit had been longer and that Becky hadn't gone and ruined everything by refusing to let Aunt Maggie adopt her baby. Becky was like Ma in some ways, stubborn to the core. Whenever she made her mind up about something, she rarely changed it.

"Stay out of trouble," Aunt Maggie said as she hugged me.

"Thank you," I whispered back, hoping she would know that I appreciated her not squealing on me to Ma the other day, and for not trying to find out where I'd really gone.

"Be sure to send more clippings," I said, and Aunt Maggie promised she would. The train whistle blew as it slowed down and Aunt Maggie picked up her bag. As I watched her board the train that day, I felt a tug at my heart. Aunt Maggie would never know how close she came to being a mother, and that thought made me a little sad.

# Chapter Twelve

"Maybe Canada won't have to go to war," I said one evening near the beginning of September. It was right after we'd got word that Britain and France had declared war on Germany. While I didn't believe countries should be fighting, I also knew it wasn't right, Germany invading Poland like that. But I also wondered why they couldn't just settle their differences themselves. Why involve the whole world in their mess? Ma looked up from her embroidery work and told me I was naive.

"Of course we'll be joining. We have no choice," she said, pulling the needle through the pillowcase she was working on. Her words momentarily stunned me, the conviction with which she said it, as if there was no doubt in her mind. Canada would be joining the war. It was a fact. Still, I hoped she was mistaken. There was a look of concern on her face, and although neither of us said so, I knew we were both thinking about Uncle Art. That night I lay awake looking out at the stars and wondered what war would mean for all of us. How many people we knew would end up going overseas to fight? Would some of my brothers be among them? If so, how many wouldn't come back? I fell asleep holding tight to the hope that if war was inevitable perhaps, by some miracle, it wouldn't affect us in our little corner of Nova Scotia.

My hopes were crushed on September 10th. While I was helping Ma with a new batch of diapers and gowns for an upcoming inspection at the maternity home, Canada joined in the war against Germany. We heard the announcement over the airwaves that evening. Ma's eyes had a hollow look to them; the lines on her face made her look older.

"Shut that thing off, Tulia," she said, marching up the steps. Minutes later I heard the sewing machine humming away.

—

"Did you hear, Tulia? It's official. We're at war," said Finny, catching up to me the next day on my way to school. He'd been expecting a war all along and yet he still sounded surprised.

"Yes, Finny, I heard. But I wish I hadn't." The news was all too fresh. I really didn't feel like talking about it. It was like someone slapping you in the face and you're not sure what to do next. Finny said that Prime Minister MacKenzie King took his good old time.

"Oh Finny," I told him, "no one wants war. I'm sure the Prime Minister doesn't either." At least I hoped he didn't. I only wished we could go back to a time before Germany had invaded Poland. Why did this Hitler have to be so greedy?

"Freedom costs," said Finny. "At least that's what my father says."

I knew more than I wanted to about the subject of war thanks to Finny Paul, who had been following the articles in the papers. His father had fought at Vimy Ridge and even got a medal that he kept shoved in the back of his dresser drawer *like it meant nothing to him*—Finny's words, not mine. I wondered if the medal reminded him of things he'd rather forget. It wasn't as if the folks in East Chester gave Nelson Paul any credit for being a war hero. Maybe war is something that gets stuck inside you, and not just you but your whole family, the same way Becky's predicament would affect all of us if folks found out the truth. As much as I didn't want to admit it, Ma was right when it came to that.

While Nelson Paul never talked about the war, that never stopped Finny. I used to tell him he was obsessed, that war had happened years ago and there was no sense talking about it now.

"I'm going to join up, Tulia," Finny said as we neared the schoolhouse, "but don't you tell anyone."

"Oh Finny, the war will be over before you're old enough

to go." At least I hoped it would be. I had no patience for his silly talk. "Shooting people isn't like shooting rats down at the dump."

"Someone's got to stop him." Finny spoke as though he would singlehandedly stop Hitler in his tracks. Easy to sound brave with an ocean separating you from war—something I'd never say to Finny out loud. He was planning to become a detective one day, maybe even a spy for our side if he was needed. He let me in on his plans one day at the dump right after I told him that I wanted to travel around the globe. Neither of us laughed at the other's dream, even though common sense should have told us that not all dreams are realistic. We both could have listed off multiple reasons why our much-dreamed-about plans would never become reality, but we didn't. Everyone should have a safe place to share their dreams without being laughed at. Maybe that was why Finny and I were such good friends.

"I saw your sister again," said Finny. "She's getting big." I grabbed Finny by the arm and stopped him before he could take another step. I didn't want anyone mentioning her name.

"You won't tell, will you?" If this got out, Becky's reputation would be destroyed.

"I'm not going to say anything, Tulia. You should know better than to ask." He was right, I should have known better.

"I didn't mean anything, it's just that Ma would never

live it down—if it got out, that is. Why are you still hanging out around the maternity home anyway?"

Before Finny could answer, there came a sudden thumping of feet behind us. Some of the boys were shouting at one another, pushing and shoving playfully as they came running toward the schoolhouse. Guy Leary and Kevin Bush were in the group. I didn't much care for either one of them. I'd known Guy since the second grade and Kevin had moved to East Chester during the summer.

"Hey Fin, don't tell me they let you off the reservation again," said Kevin, slapping Finny on the back. I saw Finny cringe beneath Kevin's touch.

"You'd better not mess with Finny or he'll take his tomahawk after you," said Guy, grinning widely.

Placing his hand on Finny's shoulder, Kevin said, "You didn't bring your tomahawk to school, did you, Finny?" Breaking out into laughter, they raced into the schoolhouse.

"One of these days, Tulia, he's going to get a fist in the mouth," Finny said. I could see the anger rising in him, and it took a lot to make Finny angry. It was understandable, the way Kevin and Guy had been running on him lately. Still, what good would it do to start a fight?

"Oh Finny," I said, hoping to lighten the mood, "they're not worth getting in trouble over."

# Chapter Thirteen

The tangled mass of branches above me moaned like a woman in labour. To my right, a web of wind chimes tinkled softly in the breeze. The music might have seemed pleasing to me had Finny Paul not told me that a girl from the maternity home had hung herself from the very same oak tree the wind chimes now dangled from. At the time, Ma said Finny should have his ears boxed for making up such an unbelievable story, because Mrs. Young would never have let a thing like that happen. *She cares about her girls*—Ma was always adamant about that. She was equally adamant when she said that Finny Paul was nothing but a troublemaker and that I should stay as far away from him as I could get.

As we started down a small footpath that November evening, I could hear muffled voices from inside the maternity home. All I could think of was what we'd do if we got caught for trespassing. We had no business being on private property, and the Youngs were about as private as any two people could be, even while being in the public eye the way they were. Yet even with the uncertainties I was feeling inside, some unexplainable force urged me on.

When I snuck out of the house earlier that evening Ma was in the sewing room stitching a dress for Cynthia Cross, who'd put in a last-minute rush on a dress to wear to her niece's wedding.

"A December wedding?" Mrs. Featherstone clucked her tongue the day Ma stopped in to buy some thread.

"It's been in the planning for months—not that Cynthia seemed to notice. She always lets things go." Ignoring Mrs. Featherstone's insinuations, Ma examined the colour and quality of the thread lined up in front of her. She was choosey that way. Things needed to be perfect.

"The invitations went out in October," she added. Picking out a spool of the finest thread in the store, she set it on the counter. Under normal circumstances she would have told Mrs. Cross that it was too short-notice, maybe even sputtered about her audacity in thinking she had nothing better to do with her time than cater to rich folks, but with a war on and the Depression still at our heels, there wasn't as much call for seamstresses in these parts, not like there once was. Even with her job at the maternity home, Ma couldn't turn down the work. Not to mention, Cynthia promised to pay her extra because of how quickly she needed it.

The full moon was already visible, the sky fading into a curtain of grey as evening closed in around us. The breeze had a bite to it. I shivered, wishing I'd dressed in a few more layers. "Can we just get this over with?" I asked, teeth chattering.

From inside the walls of the maternity house came a series of high-pitched screams. I turned quickly toward Finny, suddenly wishing I'd stayed home. Coming here had been a mistake.

"We should just leave," I said, shaking off the icy finger tapping at my spine.

"Don't tell me you're scared," he said as if reading my mind. Finny was fearless and that sometimes frightened me. With all the ribbing he was getting from Kevin and Guy, I feared what would happen one day. Finny would only take so much.

"I'm not scared. I just don't want to get caught," I said, which was only half true. I shouldn't have promised to come look in the shed in the first place.

"We're not going until we see what Mr. Young put in here this morning," he said, moving toward the small building behind the maternity home. I'd hoped with his interest in the war, he'd give up spying on the Youngs. But Finny rarely gave up on things.

Dusk hurried us on. Soon we wouldn't be able to see a hand in front of us, which made me question what we would see inside the toolshed this time of evening anyway. My muscles tensed with a readiness that would send me into a sprint should someone suddenly appear. I looked back over my shoulder. A silhouette from upstairs shifted behind a veil of lacy white sheers. More screams followed. Downstairs, someone moved toward the window and pulled the curtain back. I squeezed into the shadow cast by the shed, trying to make myself invisible while the yelling and screaming continued.

"Can't you just let it go, Finny?"

Ignoring my protests, he pulled back his shoulders and said, "It's in here."

"Just hurry," I whispered, knowing it was useless to argue with him. Finny opened the door and three large strides put him on the other side of the shed. I followed close behind, steered by fear and morbid curiosity. Finny stepped aside and I leaned in for a closer look. The only object on the table was a wooden butterbox. Finny gently removed the lid. I held my breath and pushed my mind out of the dark corner it had crawled into. When I bent down closer to the table, a gasp slipped out of me. Even with the light being as pale as what it was, I could tell there was something inside the box: a tiny body, cold and lifeless. I pulled back in horror.

"Let's get out of here," I said quickly.

"But Tulia. Someone should know. You said yourself no one will listen to me."

"And so you think I'm the one to report this? Who would I tell, anyway?"

"Your ma works here. I thought—"

"Exactly. She works here, and if they get shut down she'll have nothing but the sewing she takes in. Finny, sometimes you have to trust that people are doing the right thing."

"You mean like Hitler? People let him do what he wanted, and look what happened there."

"Look, this doesn't involve you or me, Finny Paul. We've got no business butting in. There could be any number of reasons why they haven't buried the poor thing yet. Stop looking to make trouble."

I turned to escape through the open door. The chilled November air made me dizzy, but I wasn't sticking around for whatever was to follow. I looked back toward the maternity home as the sounds inside grew louder. I was reminded of the day Donna's baby was born. My legs trembled but I forced myself to keep moving. It didn't take long for Finny to have the shed door secured and I could hear his feet scuffing against the gravel stones behind me.

And then someone was yelling, *"Push...Debbie. Push, for the love of God, push. Won't you?"* I stopped in my tracks. My heart made a quick jump. Debbie—the name Mrs. Young gave to Becky. But Becky's baby wasn't due for another three weeks. I quickly looked at Finny.

"What's wrong?" he asked.

"Finny, that's Becky screaming," I said, looking toward

the maternity home.

"Are you sure?"

I nodded.

*"Push, Debbie, push!"*

*"I can't do this no more!"*

*"Of course you can do it. Now push! Puuuush!"*

And then the air drained of all sound. Seconds later, the wind whipped the muffled cries of a baby in our direction—a sound so faint and tattered I wasn't sure if it was coming from inside the house or if some ghostly force outside the home was making its presence known. The cries became swallowed up by the tinkling of the wind chimes. A part of me wanted to rush into the maternity home to be with Becky, but instead I turned toward home.

"Come on, Finny," I said, pulling on his arm.

"Are you sure?"

"I'm sure." There was nothing I could do for Becky. My mind was on our front door and the warmth from the stove in the good room, the smell of baked apples that I knew would still be lingering in the air from supper—and Ma.

We didn't utter a word all the way home, something that was totally out of character for Finny. I thought he'd try to convince me that the Youngs were up to no good, but he didn't. From our front stoop, I could see that the light was still on in the sewing room.

Turning to Finny, I made a final plea. "You've got to stop

all this, Finny Paul. It doesn't matter, none of it. You've got to let it go." No good would come from his snooping around the maternity home, I was sure of it.

"Tell that to the dead baby in the shed. Tell its mother it doesn't matter. See what she tells you." There was more expression in his voice than I might have expected.

"You don't even know who the mother is. She's nothing to you. Babies die, Finny. They have since the beginning of time. Don't make this into something it's not." I sounded like Ma, but I couldn't help myself. Someone had to talk some sense into him. His obsession with the maternity home didn't seem natural for a boy his age. What made him care so much?

"It's not right, Tulia—you know that yourself. And someone's got to put a stop to it."

"It's not for you or me," I said, the child in me wanting nothing more than to ignore the events surrounding this entire evening. "If it wasn't for the Youngs we'd be living at the poor farm, Ma and me. You know that. Now go, Finny Paul. I got to stay out of it." I pushed on his shoulders, determined that he leave.

"But—"

"I've got nothing more to say on it, Finny. Nothing." I folded my arms across my body. I was ready to put this to subject to rest. I watched him leave, a dark figure fading into the dusk.

The soft purr of Ma's treadle sewing machine met

me at the door. She'd been so absorbed in her work she hadn't realized I was gone. I swallowed a gulp of air as I struggled to hold back the tears building inside me. I wanted to rush into the sewing room and tell Ma that Becky had her baby, but I couldn't do that. I was dying to know if Becky was all right, if the baby was all right. I'd heard its cries, so that was a good sign. Hanging my coat up, I quietly climbed the stairs and got ready for bed.

"Goodnight, Ma," I called out as I pulled back the quilts and climbed between the sheets. The sewing machine didn't lose the rhythm Ma had settled into as she answered back, "Sleep tight." Hard as I tried to push the events of the evening from my mind, I couldn't. I shouldn't have gone out to the maternity home. I knew no good would come from it.

Reaching for the scrapbook on my dresser, I lay in bed absently flipping through the pages. I couldn't stop thinking about Becky's baby. If it was a boy the Merrys would adopt him, but if it was a girl...I didn't want to even think about it. But whether it was a girl or a boy, I knew one thing for sure: I'd probably never get to hold my niece or nephew. Not even once.

I fell asleep looking at the clippings, Ma's sewing machine comforting me with its steady rhythm as she worked long into the night.

# Part Two

1940

## Chapter Fourteen

⸙ *&&* ⸙

I rushed over to Becky's bedside and knelt on the floor next to her. Her blonde hair was matted and damp. She looked up at me and forced a smile. She was tired, I could tell.

"It's all over, Tulia," she said. "It wasn't so bad." A tear glistened in the corner of her eye. I didn't believe her.

"I want to go see." I was anxious to rush off to the nursery, but it only seemed polite not to hurry away.

"You can't. The Merrys were just here." It seemed strange that I didn't notice their wagon in the driveway when I arrived. Becky must be mistaken.

"The Merrys? But how did they find out so soon?" It hadn't been but a day since I'd heard Becky screaming and Mrs. Young calling out for her to push, push, puushh! Surely news didn't travel that fast.

"You can change your mind," I said, trying one last time.

"I signed papers. But it's okay, Tulia. It's okay."

Her voice was like the haunting music made by the wind chimes in the oak tree behind the maternity home. I could hardly make out her words. They had a dizzying effect on me. I stood and turned toward the door, needing fresh air. The baby was gone, taken away before I could see it.

"Look, Tulia, look what I have here," Becky called out anxiously, drawing my attention back toward her. She pulled open the quilt and I leaned in closer to see. It was a baby, but it didn't look real—a doll, maybe. Its skin was smooth and white; its eyelids were barely open. *Such a strange-looking doll*, I thought, but then suddenly realized that something was desperately wrong with it. My heart thundered in my throat. It was not a doll but the baby me and Finny found in the shed the other night. Screaming, I backed away from Becky and raced outside. The Merrys' wagon was far in the distance. I didn't know what to do, which way to turn. My heart wouldn't stop pounding.

A ray of moonlight flooded my bedroom and I sat up, panting. It was the same dream, the one that kept coming to me on Friday nights, the day before I was to go help Ma at the maternity home. I told Finny we should never have gone into the shed that night.

Reaching for my scrapbook, I pulled it onto the bed with me and imagined my trip to Quintland one day to see the Quintuplets. Hugging fast to it, I finally drifted off into sleep.

There was hardly a sound coming from the nursery, something that rarely happened at the maternity home. Usually by the time the last baby was fed and changed, another one would start to fuss. Sometimes the walls nearly vibrated from all the wailing. I used to feel sorry for the girls looking after all those babies when they were screaming for hours on end. How would you choose which one to feed first? I quietly made my way up the stairs. What little time I had with the babies were usually stolen moments when Ma was outside hanging out clothes. Ma never wanted me making a lot of the little ones.

"You'll get attached and then they'll be gone," she'd say. She was right about that. Marie got adopted out last fall. I didn't find out, not right away, with Ma ordering me to stay away from the maternity home while Becky was there. I shouldn't have been surprised to find her gone. Common sense told me it was for the best. Every baby in that nursery had to fight for any bit of attention it got. I should have been pleased to find out that Marie was being loved by a mother and father, but when I got home I cried for a couple of hours. I'd never get to hold her again.

I've heard some people say that all babies look alike. Marie had a full head of hair and soft pink lips. The impostor in her crib was practically bald and his cry was coarse.

Sally looked up as I entered the nursery and smiled. "I

was wondering if you'd be coming today," she said. There were dark rings under her eyes and her hair looked as though it could use combing. She was rocking a baby in her lap and I'd heard her softly humming as I was coming up the stairs. Sally's real name was Beth, not that I was supposed to know, and she'd been at the home since last fall. We were in town the day she stepped off the bus holding a small brown suitcase. She had the most pitiful look on her face you could imagine.

"I'm looking for Mrs. Young," she'd said, stopping us as we walked past. "Do you know where she is?"

She looked like maybe she'd burst out crying at any moment if someone didn't soon do something. Sticking her nose in the air, Ma snapped out, "How should I know?" and pulled me close to her side. Head held straight, she dug in her heels, pulling me along with her.

"The bus stops right in front of the maternity home. It's off the road, but it's big. You'll find Mrs. Young there. Next stop. You can't miss it," I called out quickly as Ma continued to yank me along.

"I'm Beth," she called out after me. I knew that wouldn't be her name for long. I didn't know many of the girls at the home; most of them hardly spoke to me. Ma wouldn't want me getting too friendly with any of them. But Sally was different. Sally was nice to everyone.

"I haven't got a lot of time. Ma's hanging out diapers," I said to Sally as I headed toward the crib by the window.

I looked in at the little baby inside. I took a deep breath, knowing she was still there—but for how long?

"She doesn't look as if she's put on an ounce in months," said Sally when she saw me bent over the crib. She's hardly but skin and bones." I wanted to pick her up but was afraid of waking her.

"Maybe she'll get adopted out soon," I said, looking down at her. I wasn't sure I wanted someone to take her away, at least not for a while yet.

"I doubt that. There's something wrong with her eyes. Mrs. Young said just the other day that she's probably blind—poor thing."

The baby began to stir, and I reached in to take her. Her eyes were smaller than most babies', but Mrs. Young was wrong. I knew she wasn't blind. If Mrs. Young paid any attention to her at all she'd have known that too. The baby could look at me and smile when I made silly faces. And it wasn't just gas the way some people say when a baby grins at them. It was an honest-to-goodness smile. To me, she was a sweetheart.

"People want perfect babies," I overheard Mrs. Young once say. "It might sound cruel, but it's the truth."

I held the baby against my cheek. If no one wanted her, did that mean she would end up at the orphanage when she got older? I didn't even want to think that way.

Standing beside the window, I swayed gently back and forth with her in my arms. Two large strings of diapers were flapping and billowing in the wind below me. Ma was struggling to pin the diapers in place. Her basket was nearly empty. I thought suddenly of the day she caught Finny snooping around the maternity home and chased him away. I wondered what she thought now that Mr. Young had hired him to help old Joe spruce up the grounds. Today was Finny's first day. I could see him following old Joe, who was several strides ahead of him. He looked to be talking as he trailed behind, pushing a wheelbarrow full of dirt. I wondered what he was saying to old Joe. Was he asking him if the rumours were true, that some of the dead babies ended up dumped into the cove?

A big piece of ground had been ploughed up last week for a vegetable garden and there were lots of shrubs to trim and flowers to weed. Not that Finny was all that interested in gardening. What he really wanted was to keep watch on the goings-on at the home. I thought what had happened back in November might discourage him, but it only made him more determined to get to the truth.

I continued to sway back and forth with the baby in my arms and her eyes slowly closed. I kissed the top of her golden head.

"Sleep tight, Cammie," I whispered. I'd seen the name in a *Star Weekly* magazines one time. It seemed to fit her perfectly.

"You have a way with her," Sally said, smiling as I settled

Cammie back in her crib. I don't know why, but I found myself fighting back tears as I made my way to the laundry room.

# Chapter Fifteen

"Old Joe doesn't do a lot of talking," said Finny as we made our way through the piles of garbage out at Lancaster's. "He mostly just grunts when I ask him things. It's not going to be easy to get him to talk about the Youngs."

"Ever think that some people don't like to yak all the time the way you do, Finny Paul?" I said, smiling. I'd given up the notion of talking him out of his plan to shut down the maternity home. Once Finny got an idea into his head, you couldn't pry it out with a crowbar. Besides, I very much doubted that Finny stood a chance of doing what those government men failed to do with all those months of inspections and paperwork. Surely the Youngs were doing something right, or else they'd have been put out of business a long time ago. As for all the talk that was going around, Ma was probably right when she said people like to stir up trouble.

The sun had been playing a game of peek-a-boo since we got there, dropping behind a cloud one minute and beaming out bright and sunny the next. It was late April so most of the leaves hadn't yet pushed their way out, but the poplar trees were beginning to bud. Ma said that was the sign of an early spring.

Ma was at her Women's Institute meeting. They were making bandages to send overseas.

I had the day to myself, as I expected she'd be gone late into the afternoon. I was in no hurry to get home and start knitting. Not that I didn't want the soldiers to be warm; knitting the scarves was easy, but I'd yet to master capping a sock heel.

"Don't worry, Tulia," Ma would say when she noted my frustration. "By the time the war is over you'll be knitting with your eyes closed." I hoped the war wouldn't last long enough for that to happen.

From somewhere on the other side of the enormous mound of garbage came the distinct shot from someone's .22. Another rat must have tumbled over into the dirt.

"Do you think you'll like working out there?" I asked.

Ignoring my question, Finny picked up an old picture frame.

"What do you think? Any good?" he said, holding it up for my inspection. Most of the plaster had chipped away, revealing the wood beneath, and one corner was jutting upward, the tiny nails having pulled apart. Finny gave it a crack with the palm of his hand to try and jar it back into place. He held it up again. It still looked crooked.

"It's seen better days. What would you use it for, anyway? Do you have a picture to fit it?" I asked.

"I guess you're right," he said, flipping it into the rubble. Another shot rang out. "Oh, and about the gardening work, I never did much weeding and planting before. Mom usually does all that, but I guess it's okay work."

"Look at it this way, Finny. You not only have a job, you're also helping the war effort." I thought it might encourage him to know he was doing more than just planting and weeding. He was still talking about enlisting in the army, but there were plenty of other things he could do that didn't involve putting himself in danger. He was still a kid. At fourteen, he wasn't old enough to join up anyway. Hopefully the war would be long over before he was.

"War effort? Now, how do you figure that?" he said, looking at me as if I was off my rocker.

"Because they want us to grow our own food. Even folks in the city are planting Victory Gardens, and that means more food can be sent overseas to the troops. And just think about all the food those women and babies at the maternity home go through. There's plenty to be done here at home. Not everyone can join in the fighting. But it all helps. I'm knitting scarves and socks." In her last letter, Aunt Maggie told us she was working in a munitions factory and that she'd ripped her lawn up and planted seeds. She said it made her feel useful. We were still waiting to hear when Uncle Art would be going overseas.

"I didn't take the job to help the war effort," Finny said.

"I know, but maybe it's like killing two birds with one stone, or maybe three, because you're getting paid too. Hey, and look," I said, swatting him on the arm with excitement, "you can buy some War Saving Stamps with your money."

Miss Forrester told us all about the stamps and how we could bring our money to school to get them. Although I was saving the money I made working in the laundry for my trip to Quintland, I figured I could spare some dimes and nickels for stamps. It only seemed right, and I didn't want to be the only girl in school to not buy any. I had filled one booklet and was starting on another. Ma seemed pleased. Besides, I'd be able to cash them in after the war. It's not like I wouldn't get the money back.

Finny shook his head and went right on talking, steering the conversation back to old Joe and the maternity home. "Old Joe—he seems like an all right fellow. A little bit strange. Did you know there are graves in the field out back of the home?"

I sighed. When was Finny going to stop all this? "And did you know you have a wild imagination?" Sometimes I did wonder where he came up with all these things.

"It's true, Tulia. Old Joe even said. He acted like it was

no big deal. 'You might have to dig a grave from time to time,' he said, like it was nothing." Finny pulled a long metal rod out of the garbage pile and threw it off to the side. Pit Croft had been gathering up scrap metal to be sent off for making machine guns. Ma cleaned out some of the old pots and pans that had been in the house since she moved in and gave them to him. Everyone we knew was doing what they could for the war. *It's all part of our patriotic duty*—Ma's words, not mine.

"There are bound to be babies dying," I said, kicking at some of the rubble. "That happens even in hospitals." Finny digging a tiny grave? Although I didn't say so, it didn't sound right.

"It's kind of creepy, having a cemetery in your back-yard." It surprised me to hear him admit that. He looked over at me, maybe realizing what he'd said. Finny liked to appear tough. I saw it many times when the other boys were ragging on him in the schoolyard. He cleared his throat. "I mean, all those babies dying. There's got to be dozens of graves by the looks of it, maybe more." He moved aside an old wooden rack, looking for more scrap metal.

Our conversation stopped suddenly when we both saw a piece of rusty metal hidden under the pile of garbage. Finny began moving things aside until he was able to reach it. We pulled on it until it came free.

"How many guns do you think this will make?" I said,

pleased with our find. A sudden trouncing of feet made me look off in the distance. Two people were heading our way, shouting. My heart dropped when I saw who it was. They were both carrying .22s.

"Let's get out of here, Finny." I didn't want trouble. Guy and Kevin were quickly approaching. My mind told me to run, but it was too late for that.

"Look, there's Tulia and her Indian boyfriend," said Guy, stopping in front of us. "What are you two doing out there? Want to borrow my .22 and get yourself some supper, Indian boy?"

"I wouldn't waste my bullets," said Kevin. They looked at one another and laughed. I hated Kevin's bucktooth grin even more than I despised Guy's floppy ears and pointy nose. They were the homeliest boys in school, not because of their looks but because of the ugliness that was inside them. I wished Kevin had never moved to East Chester. Together, they were a dangerous combination. It was rumoured they had vandalized Ted Parker's fence last month and broken the windows out of Mr. Collicutt's workshop.

"What's it to you what we're doing here?" said Finny, stepping toward Guy. The way he said it made me think he was going to punch Guy in the face, that and the clenched fist he was holding tightly at his side.

I pulled on Finny's arm. "Come on. It's not worth it," I said. Finny's breathing was laboured and his muscles were tense. I didn't want them to get into a brawl. Two against one didn't seem the least bit fair.

"Yeah, come on, chicken," mocked Guy, poking Finny in the chest. "Gonna run home to Mommy, are you?" I could feel Finny resisting as I pulled on his arm. He shook me off like he was ready for a fight. There was fire in his eyes. I'd never seen him look so angry.

"Think I'm scared of you?" he said, not backing down an inch.

"Please, Finny," I pleaded. It wasn't worth him getting the daylight beat out of him. Kevin was big and rugged. Everyone knew he was the one responsible for beating up Eric Conrad last month, even though Eric wouldn't tell. Why wouldn't Finny just walk away?

Just then, a rumbling of wheels drew our attention toward the entrance to the dump. I was never so thankful to see Pit Croft's old bald head in all my life. I could have run over and kissed it.

"Come on, Kevin. Let's get out of here," said Guy as Pit's truck came nearer.

"Yeah," agreed Kevin, snarling as he looked Finny in the eye. "I've got better things to do than to fight some worthless Indian." They hurried off. My knees were still a bit wobbly as Pit's truck pulled up and stopped. He rolled down his window.

"Nice morning," he said with a wrinkled smile. "Thought I'd come look for some scrap."

"Finny found a pipe and we just pulled out a big piece from the pile," I said, pointing to our finds.

"Every bit helps the effort," said Pit. He climbed out of his truck and hobbled toward the metal we had set aside. Someone said a piece of shrapnel hit him in the leg when he was fighting in the last war.

"It sure does," agreed Finny. He gave Pit a smile and pick up one of the pieces of metal we'd found. Finny looked about back to normal and I was glad for that. One thing about Finny, he didn't hang on to his anger for long.

# Chapter Sixteen

⸺ ❧ ⸺

"I thought the Merrys were going to bring the baby out to visit sometime," I said to Ma one evening while we were knitting in the parlour. It was the beginning of May and we hadn't seen the baby, not once. It was only fair that we should, since Ma promised we'd get to see him back when all the plans were being made. I was beginning to wonder if she hadn't said all that to shut me up. It had been months and so far we hadn't laid eyes on him. Christmas came and went. I thought she might quilt him a blanket and mail it off, but she didn't.

"We can't very well be sending the child gifts. Ethel will think I'm butting in," she said, yanking out a length of yarn before continuing her knitting. Ma wasn't fooling me. I knew how these things worked. First, a year would go by, and then another. He'd be grown up before we knew it. Her resistance didn't make sense to me. Wasn't she the least bit curious to see her own grandson?

"It's not as if we haven't seen him," she said, her needles clicking softly together as she spoke. I thought about his round, chubby cheeks and the fuzzy brown hair on his head. I didn't even get to hold him.

"We saw him once and he was only a day old and then you took him out to the Merrys without me."

"And that's precisely why I wouldn't let you go. I knew how you'd carry on," she said as I continued to complain about how unfair she was being.

"We're never going to see him," I finally said out of frustration.

"Oh Tulia, stop your nonsense. I'm sure they'll come by once the weather warms up," said Ma, looking up from her knitting. The yarn she was using was from an old brown sweater that once belonged to Daddy. I ravelled it out last February during a big snowstorm. Ma said it would likely make three or four pairs of socks. "The Merrys don't own a vehicle. You can't very well expect them to bring a baby this far in a wagon, especially this time of the year. Why, the poor little thing would catch his death of cold."

"We have a car. Why can't we go there?" Ma sent me a disapproving look. It seemed a sensible request, so I kept at her. "Why not, Ma? We take the car to Chester when we need to go." Usually to run errands for Mrs. Young, I could have added, but didn't, and when we needed to pick up chicken feed at the Co-op. "So why can't we go to Tanner?"

"Tanner's a lot farther away than Chester, as you well know." Her needles began to pick up speed. I could usually tell when she was displeased at something by how fast her needles were moving. Right now, she was only mildly annoyed.

I saw my chance and got in a quick, "But Ma," before she cut me off.

"The Merrys need time to get settled in with the baby and we should respect that. For now, we have no right to interfere." Ma got a letter from Mrs. Merry the other day but it said very little, only that he was growing quickly and was a happy baby. She also expressed her undying gratitude...again.

*We are ever so grateful to you for arranging this and cannot fully put into words how we feel about this most precious gift you have given us. Quite simply, he is the light of our lives.*

It was nice to know that Mrs. Merry finally got the baby she'd been wanting for years, but I was dying to see him for myself. I was sure it wouldn't happen anytime soon.

Ma pulled out another length of yarn and went back to her knitting. Her needles had slowed down a little.

"Now get back to work, Tulia May, and stop all this foolishness. Some poor soldier's going to need a warm scarf when the weather gets cold. We'll sort all this out later. Right now we've got work to do. There's a war on. We need to do our part."

Miss Forrester clapped her hands together to get everyone's attention. Someone burped and everyone laughed. Through pink cheeks, she kept talking.

"I'm going to pass around some lined paper and I want each and every one of you to write a letter to a soldier overseas," she said.

She walked between the desks setting a sheet of stationery in front of each one of us, as a chorus of moans and groans passed through the schoolhouse. I looked down at the blank page in front of me. I'd only ever written letters to Aunt Maggie. Miss Forrester's fiancé had gone overseas in December and they had to postpone their wedding. Maybe she thought one of our letters would reach him.

"But Miss Forrester, I don't know how to write a letter," whined Jimmy Bowers. I'd be surprised if Jimmy could write anything other than his name, same as the other students in the primary class.

"You and the rest of the primaries may draw pictures," she said, placing a blank sheet of paper in front of the younger kids. "I'm sure the soldiers will enjoy seeing your artwork. This is for the students who have studied letter writing, and even if you haven't I want you to all take part. Anyone who needs help, put up your hand."

"I don't see the point in writing to some stranger I've never seen before, Miss Forrester," said Catherine, flipping her hair behind her shoulder. It was as if she could read my mind.

"Imagine being a soldier, away from your family. Imagine never knowing if this day will be your last. Imagine the loneliness you're feeling. Perhaps you're even homesick if you haven't been away from your family before. Some of these soldiers aren't much older than some of you," said Miss Forrester, making her way to the front of the class. "Now, imagine receiving a letter or a parcel from back home. It might just brighten your day." I wondered if her fiancé was feeling lonely and homesick.

Someone released a heavy sigh. I stared down at the blank page on my desk wondering what to write. What would I say to someone on the other side of the Atlantic, someone I didn't even know? Miss Forrester said we should write about the happenings in our lives, but I knew that wasn't possible. I knew the weather would make for some pretty uninteresting reading. There was the spring dance that was coming up, but that didn't seem to me like something a soldier would care to read about. I couldn't write about any of the happenings at the maternity home; our aim was to cheer up the soldiers, not make them sad.

I looked across the aisle. Both Hope and Marlee had their heads down, writing. I didn't want to look clueless. I had to come up with something, and quick. *Write about something that interests you*, Miss Forrester had said, and then it dawned on me. I suddenly knew what to write.

*Dear Mr. Soldier,*

*Have you ever heard of the Dionne quintuplets?*

*My name is Tulia May Thompson. I am thirteen years old and I live in East Chester, Nova Scotia.*

From there I knew exactly what to write. I started out by saying that I was very keen when it came to the Dionne quintuplets and that I had a scrapbook filled with photos of them. I was even so bold as to say I probably knew more about them than their own parents. I said how they were born on May 10, 1934, near Callander in Northern Ontario, and that they were so small the doctor who delivered them didn't think they would live. I wrote how their names were Cecile, Marie, Annette, Yvonne, and Emilie and that they lived in a place called Quintland. I even added that I planned to visit there one day.

After I had written all the things I knew about the world-famous quintuplets, I sealed the letter in an envelope and handed it to Miss Forrester. I really did hope my letter would brighten some soldier's day. With so many people going off to war, maybe it would find its way to someone I knew, maybe even someone like Uncle Art.

# Chapter Seventeen

⌒—888—⌒

We followed behind the Youngs' car to Fox Point in the early morning. Ma said it was okay for me to take a few hours off from school, that she'd write a note for Miss Forrester. I wondered what that note would say, since Mrs. Young demanded privacy for all her girls. I was pretty sure that meant the dead ones, too. What excuse would Ma come up with to explain my absence? A funeral wasn't something to be passed over without question in a small place like East Chester. There would be a list of whos and wheres and hows to answer to.

I fiddled with the buttons on the navy jacket I was wearing, trying to keep my mind off where we were going. Aunt Maggie gave me the jacket last summer when she came to visit. It was *gently used*—Aunt Maggie's words, not mine, but it was probably the nicest jacket I'd ever get to own. The air was cold and dreary and I'd been looking for an excuse to put it on. Ma didn't believe in dressing up in good clothes for everyday, so I had yet to find a place to wear it. Wearing it to a funeral wasn't exactly what I had in mind.

I looked out my side window at the trees as we went by. They appeared dull and grey without leaves, but at least the grass was beginning to green up. Spring still seemed miles away. I was anxious to see the yellow heads of dandelions popping up through the grass. I tried to imagine cheerier things, but I couldn't stop the dreary feelings inside me. I hadn't been to a funeral since Daddy died. Most of that day I'd blocked from my memory, although I recall driving in the undertaker's car with Becky and Ma, us pulling up to the church—and roses. I remember the overpowering scent of roses that met us inside the church. We were most of us there, my brothers and sisters with their wives and husbands and my cousins, the ones who lived close enough to come; so many of us that we filled one side of the church. Today, there was to be only four of us besides the undertaker. Mrs. Young was right, that seemed a shame.

Ma kept twisting her hands on the steering wheel as we drove along. My brain felt half-numb and I couldn't think of a single thing worth talking about. When she hit a pothole I didn't cry out like I normally would have. As rough and muddy as what the road was, it would be nearly impossible not to hit the occasional hole. I couldn't blame Ma's driving that time.

Ma had no plans on going to the service, but Mrs. Young could be persuasive when she wanted to be. She came to our house and asked us to come. She told Ma that the poor girl was mostly alone in the world except for a sister that hadn't yet been located and perhaps never would be. Ma happened to be working the day Eunice died. I could tell something had happened when I got home from school by the look on her face. At first she denied it but then she made me swear on the Bible that I wouldn't breathe a word of what she was about to tell.

"Someone should be there for that poor soul," said Mrs. Young last evening. "If you could spare an hour of your time, Naomi. What's one hour out of an entire lifetime?" Ma finally agreed that, yes, someone should go, and that it was the right thing to do. Before she left, Mrs. Young turned quickly and added, "And by all means, bring Tulia," like I didn't have an ounce of say in the matter.

"Will there be another trial?" I finally asked as we drove along, breaking the silence that seemed louder than my words. It wasn't at all what I'd wanted to say, but I thought it would sound shallow of me to talk about how Catherine Haley had bought five booklets of War Stamps—the most of anyone in the school.

"The baby was premature," said Ma. "Eunice went into labour early. There was nothing that could be done to prevent the outcome. No one is arguing that point." Ma sounded firm in her conviction. I could only hope she was right.

"But what about Eunice?" It seemed wrong not using her real name, but Mrs. Young was the only one who knew that.

"Her heart; the doctor concurred," said Ma, staring straight at the road ahead.

"Her heart?" I said, swallowing the word. She wasn't very old—none of the girls were.

"Apparently she was born with a defect. One of those things that go undetected." Ma seemed to have all the answers. While I expect death was an inevitable part of operating a maternity home, mothers didn't usually die there—except in the Flemming case, that is.

Ma swore me to secrecy and I had no intentions of telling another living soul what had happened to Eunice, but the hardest part about all of this would be keeping it from Finny Paul. He'd twist it into something evil if I told him. Finny didn't understand the way things worked. Mrs. Young promised privacy. *Mother's Refuge—No Publicity*, the ads in the newspaper said. It was why people came to the Ideal Maternity Home in the first place. There was secrecy involved around the babies at the home; there always had been. Whether one died or was adopted out, no one knew for sure. I only found out that Marie got adopted out because Sally was there when the people picked her from the nursery.

"They seemed like a lovely couple," she told me the day I discovered that Marie was gone. It was meant to make me feel better, but it didn't.

The hearse was at the cemetery when we pulled up. Some men dressed in black were walking across the green turf. A pine coffin was already in place. The Youngs got out of their car and Mr. Young hurried on ahead. He was a quiet man with little to say. He was more like a shadow that moved about the home, hardly seen yet you knew he was there. Mrs. Young stood in the road looking back at us. Ma mumbled something under her breath and opened the car door.

"Come on, Tulia," she ordered. I sighed. There was no way to get out of this.

"The minister's waiting," said Mrs. Young, walking back to join us. She looped her arm around Ma's and they walked down the road side by side. They were a strange sight, Mrs. Young towering over Ma, who was barely five feet tall.

"They'll go off to Glory together," Mrs. Young explained as we neared the open grave. The minister looked up with his prayer book open.

"We're ready," said Mrs. Young, and the minister began to speak.

That night I dreamed about the baby in the shed again. I woke up panting and gasping.

# Chapter Eighteen

Ma grabbed for her handbag and took a quick peek in the hallway mirror.

"Don't forget to bring your poster along," she said as she went out the door. I sighed; it seemed like she was always one step ahead of me. Rushing back upstairs, I grabbed the poster off my bed and hurried toward the car. By that time, Ma already had the car started and was revving the motor with impatience. Laying the poster on the back seat, I climbed in the front and slammed the car door shut. It was a perfect day for a drive and I suddenly felt full of adventure. What was the good of us having a car if we couldn't use it to have a little fun now and again?

"Let's take a drive down to Lunenburg," I said, looking over at Ma. She let out a grunt and adjusted the rear-view mirror as if it would need adjusting. She was the only one who ever drove the car.

"Need I remind you that there's a war on, and we're expected not to go gallivanting around, burning up gasoline for frivolous matters? Nor do I think Mrs. Young would appreciate our sporting around Lunenburg in her car. No...Chester's far enough for us."

"The car's all yours, Ma. Mrs. Young gave it to you. You don't need her permission. Besides, it was just sitting around gathering rust." Seemed like I was always reminding her of that fact. With the offer of the car, there came certain strings attached; Ma being expected to run errands whenever Mrs. Young was too busy happened to be one of those strings. Mrs. Young was a shrewd one, no two ways around it.

"That's no excuse for taking advantage," said Ma.

"Oh Ma, haven't you ever just wanted to kick up your heels and let loose?" I wasn't ready to let the subject drop. I'd asked Ma about driving to Lunenburg several times in the past and it always ending with her telling me the same thing. Although I knew what the answer would be before I'd even asked, I couldn't stop thinking that maybe one day she'd make a slip and come out with *That sounds like a wonderful idea, Tulia May. We can walk along the waterfront and have lunch downtown in one of those fancy little eating establishments.* Not that I'd survive the shock if she ever did.

"Kick up my heels. What's that supposed to mean?" she grunted.

"You know, kick up your heels. Have a little fun." I

looked over at her but she seemed unmoved. I sighed. "Haven't you ever wanted to have fun for once in your life, Ma?"

"You can help pick out some lace for your dress. How's that for kicking up your heels?"

"Oh Ma," I said, crossing my arms at my chest.

"Don't 'oh Ma' me. You'll want to look presentable at the dance," she said, as if she thought I wouldn't notice how smoothly she'd changed the subject. If Aunt Maggie were here, I bet Ma would have been more than happy to go out driving. *Aunt Maggie*—I felt a queasiness in the pit of my stomach thinking of Uncle Art waiting to go overseas.

"The Jeffersons got some new lace in last week," she continued.

My appearance at the spring dance always weighed more heavily on Ma's mind than it ever did mine. She was determined that I should always be the best-dressed girl there. It was a matter of pride for her. Ma was the best seamstress for miles around and she planned for people to remember it, too. With the Depression and then the war, folks were hanging on to what few pennies they had, but she expected that one day things would straighten out and the sewing business would pick up again. "It's not like wearing clothes is going to go out of fashion," she often said. People would remember her fine work.

When I didn't jump at her suggestion, she said, "Can't

you muster up a little excitement, seeing how half the town will be at the dance?" Putting the car in reverse, she added, "I don't see why you can't be like the other girls your age."

"What, and make a fool of myself like Catherine Haley and that crowd always chasing after the boys? If I went on the way they did you'd tell me to grow up." Marlee and Hope said it was a lost cause for the three of us anyway. I didn't tell them that I wasn't interested in dancing with any of the boys at school. I still had my sights set on Beecher Merry. I'd seen him a few months ago at Firmin Jefferson's store, and even if we never got properly introduced, I was sure the smile he sent me would keep me daydreaming about him for a lifetime.

"Oh, Tulia, they're just girls, and that's what girls do." Ma searched the floor with her left foot as she tried to find the clutch. She was not the best driver around. The first few months after she sent for her licence in the mail, I had to tell her to take her foot off the gas and slow down before she drove us in the ditch.

"There's not much to get excited over when your mother makes herself out to be one of the chaperones," I said, waiting for her to put the car in gear. "I'll be ancient before anyone asks me to dance." I knew Ma wouldn't like hearing it, but it was the truth. It was why I never cared to go to the spring dance in the first place. Every year she acted like my own personal chaperone. She'd strut around the centre with her arms crossed, looking like she was ready to haul off and clout the first boy who gave me a second look. And it wasn't as if she was ever asked to be a chaperone, but how else could I explain her presence at the dance? I had to tell my friends something or else end up looking like a loser. Everyone knew Ma wasn't the dancing kind.

"You'll get to dance," came her crusty reply. She pushed the clutch in and gripped the shifting lever, slowly backing up. The car made a few quick jerks but she managed to keep it from stalling.

"It's not the same thing. Phillip's my relation. If I die an old maid, Ma, I hope you know it'll be your fault." The thought of dancing with your nephew would be a sad prospect for any thirteen-year-old, but Ma never could understand that. Ever since my birthday in January I'd been hoping that thirteen was the magic number, the number that would tell Ma I was old enough, independent enough, and smart enough to take care of myself; to maybe go to the spring dance without her by my side and even to take the train to Ontario next summer on my own. I was still scheming with Aunt Maggie about my visit with her and hoping that the war wouldn't interfere with our plans.

"Be thankful I'm allowing you to go at all. Janet Cleaves never let poor Marianne out of her sight, and look how that ended. I used to feel sorry for that girl, always hanging off her mother's sleeve when she was growing up. Granted, she was a little backwards, but Janet not letting go of the apron strings did precious little to help that girl in the end." Braking, she searched for first gear.

"Oh Ma, Marianne Cleaves ran off with the Raleigh man as soon as she turned eighteen and you know it. She got halfways to Bridgewater before her mother even knew she was gone." Word had it they eloped that day, spent their honeymoon at the Fairview Inn on Queen's Street. They didn't come out of their room for three whole days, not even when Janet and Raymond showed up on the second day pounding at the door. I'd heard the whole story from Mrs. James at the post office, who'd heard it first-hand from Janet's second cousin from down around Mahone Bay. The last anyone heard, Marianne was living in Western Shore with a passel of babies underfoot and I could almost bet Janet Cleaves wasn't losing sleep over it, neither.

"That's enough of your smart tongue, Tulia May Thompson." When Ma finally stepped on the gas pedal, gravel and dust flew. A spray of feathers fanned the air as the old red rooster was sent squawking and running for safety. Shifting gears again she started down the road, unconcerned. In my side-view mirror, a flurry of red wings was still fluttering as Rusty took refuge on the driveway post. I was relieved to see he was still mobile.

The silence that followed was welcome. Ma never

did much talking while driving, which suited me fine. Thinking about the dance was making my irritation with her rise, but I continued to bite my tongue. I couldn't help but be annoyed with her outdated ideas. It was 1940, but Ma acted as though we'd just turned the century mark.

As we rolled into town Ma stopped down by the waterfront and got out of the car, quickly smoothing the wrinkles from her clothing. A gull screeched at us, swooping down close to the water's surface. Grabbing the poster from the back seat, I stepped out of the car and closed the door. The wind caught the poster and it flapped in my hands. The gull landed not far from where we were parked. I turned my face up toward the clouds and I thought about being twirled around the dance floor by someone I wasn't related to, maybe even Beecher Merry.

"Hurry along now, Tulia May," said Ma, snapping me out of my reverie. Pulling her handbag close to her body, she cleared her throat. "We haven't got all day, you know."

I looked toward the soaring birds, felt the sweet gentle breeze on my cheeks, and wondered what that kind of freedom would feel like.

# Chapter Nineteen

⁓ 888 ⁓

**M**r. Jefferson was rearranging cans on the shelves when we walked in the store.

"Stick it up there on the wall next to the one for the recital," he said when I asked if I could pin up a poster for the dance. Glancing up from his work, he added, "Morning, Naomi," and kept on working. Nodding, Ma took out the piece of paper Mrs. Young had given her yesterday and began picking up the items on the list.

"Can I help you, Naomi?" said Mrs. Jefferson, her shoes clicking across the floor. Ma and Mrs. Jefferson both belonged to the Women's Institute and had plenty to chat about these days. They soon settled in to talk about the war.

I looked down at the poster I was holding. It lacked any form of creativity, but I knew the people in East Chester wouldn't notice.

*What: Annual Spring Dance*
*When: Saturday, June 8, 8:30–11:30*
*Where: Community Clubhouse in East Chester*
*Come one, come all for an evening of song, dance, and*
*refreshment.*
*Music supplied by Jack Banner's Band.*

The bell above the door tinkled. As I pulled out a tack, I felt something warm on the back of my head. The faint odour of the barn and some kind of soap reached my nostrils. I whirled around and let out a gasp as the poster slipped from my fingers. It was Beecher Merry. Smiling, he retrieved the poster from the floor and handed it to me. Later, as I thought it though in my head, I was almost sure I'd heard harp music playing somewhere in the background.

"Sounds like fun," he said. He must have seen the confusion on my face. I had no idea what he was talking about even though my brain was screaming for me to say something without sounding like an idiot.

"Fun...you know...the dance," he said, nodding down at the poster that was now trembling in my fingers.

"Oh, yeah, fun," I said, frantically searching for something witty to say, like maybe asking him if he was going to the dance, for starters. My heart was beating fast and furious. I was sure he could hear. This was the chance

I'd been waiting for, wishing for, dreaming about—why couldn't I get some sensible words to come out of my mouth? I stood there blankly until he asked if I was planning to go. Finally I managed to say, "I...er...I...yes." My legs felt as though they were going to let me down. The spell broke when the bell above the door tinkled again. We both looked toward the sound. Jim Merry stuck his head in through the door. I felt suddenly ashamed, me gushing over Beecher like that when his parents couldn't see fit to bring Becky's baby to see us or invite us out to their place for that matter.

"Are you about ready, Beecher?"

He cleared his throat. "In a few minutes, Pa. I'll be right there. Maybe I'll see you there. At the dance, I mean," he said, flashing me a big smile. My cheeks felt about ready to crack. I was sure I'd burst wide open from happiness. Wait until I told Hope and Marlee. They were never going to believe it. I wasn't sure how I was going to make it through the next while until the dance came around. I stood staring at him as he walked up to the counter, like he was going to evaporate at any moment.

He picked out some liquorice pipes, handed over a coin, and thanked Mr. Jefferson when he gave him back the change. A tiny tin cup on the counter caught his attention and he picked it up and examined it. "How much?" he asked Mr. Jefferson.

"Twenty-five cents."

Reaching into his pocket, he took out a quarter and placed it on the counter. "It's for my baby brother," he said, and the smile slid from my face. His baby brother—my nephew. Thinking about him made me sad all over again. When Beecher went for the door, he looked back at me and gave a nod. Jim Merry was standing in the doorway, waiting. His eyes met mine. Something strange tugged at my heart. He looked as though he was planning to smile but didn't. I couldn't help wondering if I'd ever forgive Jim Merry and his wife for taking Becky's baby from us.

We had just left the Jeffersons' store and put Mrs. Young's box of items into the car when the rumbling of bus wheels in the distance sent Ma off like a streak of greased lightning.

"The bus is coming in, Tulia May. Now come along," she said. Ma reached the dry-goods store first. Her shoe clacked against the wooden step.

"Tulia May!" she snapped, looking back at me. It wasn't as if the world would come to an end if we were there when the bus stopped. Ma was too impatient.

"I'm going to see if there's anything from Aunt Maggie first," I said, looking across the road in the direction of the post office.

Standing on the front step of the store, Ma waited for me to cross the road. As the bus went past, a curious sight stopped me in my tracks. A bright collage of red, orange, and yellow was waving out one of the windows. It was a sight filled with promises and laughter, and the giddy feelings of summer just around the bend. I'd always wanted a scarf like that, but I knew better than to want. Wants were for rich folks; easily thought up, easily gotten. Grabbed by another gust of wind, the scarf was suddenly sucked out the window. It shot up into the sky, swirling its colours around and around. I thought it would get caught up in the branches of the maple trees, but a few wild dives and it missed the trees altogether, landing in the middle of the road. It was pulled along the dirt, a good stiff wind sending it in my direction. For a moment, all I wanted to do was laugh at that silly scarf hopping across the ground.

"You mind your business and cross the road, Tulia." Ma always seemed to be watching me, no matter where I was or what I was doing.

"Oh Ma, I'm not hurting nothing. I was just looking at that scarf."

The scarf stopped about twenty feet up from the post office in the tall grass along the roadside. Another foot or so and it would have landed in the ditch. The second Ma stepped into the dry-goods store, I made a beeline toward it. Snatching it up, I shook off the dust. It felt soft and silky when I held it to my cheek and smelled strong after perfume. I had the feeling this might just be my lucky day. I shoved the scarf in my dress pocket and headed on my way. The bus squeaked to a stop just as I reached the post office. Mrs. James was sitting behind the counter when I walked in.

"Good day, Tulia," she said, quickly glancing up from the crossword she was working on.

"Yes, a very good day," I said, smiling to myself. When the most handsome guy you've ever seen practically asks you to the spring dance, and then a pretty scarf nearly lands at your feet, it can't be anything but a good day.

"Anything for Ma or me?"

Mrs. James turned to check the mail slots. "A letter from Magnolia," she said, smiling as she handed it to me. "Looks to be rather thick. She must have plenty of time on her hands to write. It's sad the way she up and moved away from here when she married Art. They never had any children, did they?" I shook my head and she made a few clucks. I squeezed the letter between my fingers. Mrs. James was right. It was thick and I was dying to rip it open, but I'd wait until I got home.

"Ella Ramey certainly got an interesting-looking parcel the other day—" The door flung open before Mrs. James could get out her next word. A woman stood in the doorway, her hand outstretched in a demanding way. She was scowling. With mousy blonde hair and green eyes, she was tough looking but in a pretty sort of way—one of those women who wouldn't stand to be pushed around.

"Where is it?" she asked, looking straight at me. There

was a wild look in her eye that told me I needed to be cautious. I had no idea what this *it* was she was talking about. The look on my face probably said as much. "It. My scarf. I saw you snitch it out of the ditch."

"I didn't snitch anything." I resented her accusation. The scarf was fair game.

"Well, the scarf isn't yours, is it?" Her head was cocked to the side, hands resting impatiently on her hips. I shook my head. "Then I call that stealing. Least, it is where I come from. Wouldn't you call that stealing?" she asked, turning her question toward Mrs. James.

Right away, I was on the defensive. I'd never stolen a thing in my life. *Finders keepers*, my mind screamed.

"I can call in the Mounted Police if you want. See what they have to say in the matter."

Mrs. James let out a squawk. Mounted Police—for a stupid scarf that probably didn't even cost half a quarter?

"Surely there's a better way to settle this," cut in Mrs. James. "If Tulia indeed has something of yours—"

"Listen, nosy, I don't recall asking for your opinion," said the woman, wagging her finger. That time, Mrs. James let out a gasp.

I pulled the scarf out of my pocket. She marched toward me and ripped it from my hand.

"Next time, don't take things that don't belong to you," she said before dashing off in the direction she came. Mrs. James and I shared a look then raced toward the door. The woman was running down the road toward the bus. Sticking our heads out the door, we heard her yelling, "Hold up. Hold up!" She ran toward the bus, wildly waving the scarf in the air. The bus started rumbling away without her in it. But she continued the chase.

"My, oh my," whispered Mrs. James, her hand to her mouth, as we stood in the doorway watching the actions unfold. This was not something that someone in Mrs. James's position should witness. Everyone who came into the post office for the next two months would hear all about this whole episode. I'd be the talk of the town—me and that strange woman with the scarf.

When it was obvious she'd missed her ride, the woman picked up a rock and threw it at the bus. It wasn't as if she could hit it from that distance, not in a million years.

"Oh dear," said Mrs. James looking over at me. "Do you suppose she's one of Lila Young's girls?"

# Chapter Twenty

My instincts told me to go find Ma. That woman at the post office had definitely lost her marbles. I headed toward the dry-goods store with no plans to relate what had just happened at the post office.

"I'll take fifty yards of white flannelette," I heard Ma say as I walked toward the back of the store. "Oh, and some cotton thread—five spools if you don't mind. Better to have too many than not enough. It'll get used eventually."

"More diapers?" clucked Mrs. Featherstone. I stroked the fabric that was lying on the cutting table, comforted by the soft, downy touch of the unwashed flannel.

"And gowns—I'll need material for gowns. Seems like everything wears out at once."

I busied myself looking for the blue taffeta I'd hidden last fall beneath the other bolts of fabric. It was the most beautiful material I'd ever seen. It made me think at the time that I wouldn't mind going to the spring dance if I had a dress made from it. The taffeta material was pricey, but Ma always put money aside to make my dress. I had been sure she'd find a way to buy it if I asked. But that was before the war. A dress made out of the blue taffeta was out of the question now.

"Sad to think that our livelihood has to come from some poor girl's misfortune," said Mrs. Featherstone as she measured off the white flannelette. "I daresay the whole community is benefiting from the business it brings our way and during these times that says a lot."

"It's the way of the world," said Ma tartly, folding the white flannelette into a neat bundle, "and not much we can do about it. There's little sense fighting it. Girls have been finding themselves in the family way since the beginning of time. I daresay there should be a silver lining somewhere."

"Will you be wanting printed material for the gowns?" Mrs. Featherstone asked, reaching for her scissors again. "New fabric came in the first of the week. Not a yard's been taken off any of the bolts."

Ma paused as if seriously considering the idea. The print material was yellow with pretty blue and pink flowers and would make beautiful gowns for any baby to wear, but Mrs. Young didn't care about any of that.

"I'd best take something more"—Ma cleared her throat—"practical. Solid yellow will do, and I'll need some extra gold embroidery floss." I sent Ma a look. I thought about the day she made the white gown for Donna's baby. They were used for burial shrouds, only she never came right out and said so. She always embroidered a small gold pair of angel wings near the neckline to help the babies fly off to heaven. She didn't get paid for those extras, but I think it made her feel better knowing it was the nicest thing those little babies were ever going to wear.

"She herds them in like cattle," Mrs. Featherstone said as she cut into the fabric with expert precision.

"They need someplace," Ma added reluctantly.

"Someplace indeed. She's far more generous than most of the population." Mrs. Featherstone made that annoying clucking sound. Ma nodded, pretending that one of her own hadn't found their way into that exact situation.

I gathered the white flannelette in my arms as Mrs. Featherstone began measuring out for the gowns. The bell at the front door jingled. Mrs. Featherstone was still prattling away when we heard someone call out, "Yoo-hoo!" Mrs. Featherstone sent us a questioning look before answering back musically, "I'll be with you in a minute." She finished measuring the material, her razor-sharp scissors cutting off the exact amount for the gowns.

"Could you make it snappy? I'm kind of in a hurry." Ma shot Mrs. Featherstone a look as if to say she couldn't believe the audacity. And then it hit me like a rock wall. I knew that voice. It belonged to that nutty woman with the scarf. My mind tried on all sorts of circumstances as to why she was in the dry-goods store. Had she followed me here? What did she want? And was she really one of Mrs. Young's girls?

"Bring it along, Tulia," Ma said once the material was cut and measured. I was still mulling over how I would get out of this scrape. Was this strange woman about to report the episode with the scarf to Ma? I followed behind Mrs. Featherstone, sinking my face into the soft fibres of flannelette.

"How can I help you?" asked Mrs. Featherstone, clearing her throat several times, something she did whenever she was annoyed.

"I need a ride out to the maternity home."

"Well then, today happens to be your lucky day," said Mrs. Featherstone, beaming a strained smile in Ma's direction. Ma's jaw clamped down tight with the force of a steel trap. I closed my eyes and swallowed.

The woman gave me a quick wink before getting in the car. She nattered away from the back seat like there were too many words inside her that kept spilling out. She said her name was Millie, but then quickly said Margaret, like she wasn't sure herself.

"Some folks call me Millie, like a nickname of sorts, but my real name's Margaret. Yes, I prefer Margaret." She went on to say she had a job waiting for her at the maternity home. Ma and I shared a look. Did this mean she *wasn't* one of Mrs. Young's girls?

"They're charging hotel rates out there, if I do say so. I'm working off my sister's bill. Brenda couldn't stay on, not in her delicate condition. Childbirth just didn't agree with her. She needed to put the whole thing behind her. Move on. That's what they say to do, isn't it—put the past behind you? I promised Nan before she died that I'd take care of my sister. That's what you do when you're the oldest, right? What difference does it make who does the work so long as the bill gets paid? That's what I told Mrs. Young. Nice country out here...look out!" she squawked. Ma swerved the car to avoid hitting Mr. Langley, who was teaming his horse and plough down the road. I grabbed for the door handle. The second we were out of danger, Margaret started up again.

Neither Ma nor I had opened our mouths since she'd climbed in back. Like a whirlwind blustering though a dry desert, she seemed to be gathering speed. I snuck a peek over at Ma. Her fingers were gripped tight to the steering wheel and her head was pointed front and centre. Ma was never good at hiding her feelings—angry feelings, that is. Leave it to Mrs. Featherstone to offer for her to drive Millie, I mean Margaret, out to the maternity home without asking first. We didn't know a thing about this woman. She could have been an escapee from a mental institution or prison for all we knew.

"Stupid bus driver took off without me. I told him to hold up when I got off. 'I'll be back in two shakes,' I said.

But did he listen? Oh, nooo. That would have been too easy for the knucklehead." She shuffled around the back seat, getting herself fired up about it all over again. I was on edge, wondering if she would blurt out the reason she'd missed the bus in the first place.

"You know, someone should see to it that he loses his job. I could have been someone important for all he knew, conducting a private investigation about bus travel and safety."

Bus travel and safety? Private investigation? She sure seemed to like the law a fair bit. "Now all I have are the clothes on my back. Son-of-a—" Ma sucked in a mouthful of air, and Margaret finished off with "sea cook, drove off with all my things. If I could get a hold of the old geezer I'd tell him a thing or two. Don't think I wouldn't."

I swallowed, still waiting for her to mention the scarf, seeing how retrieving it was the reason she'd stepped off the bus in the first place.

"That old woman from the store acted like I was from Mars or something. I haven't got two heads. What's the matter with the people around here?" She sighed. "Oh well, at any rate I got a drive out. I appreciate it."

Fighting off the need to defend every last person within a fifty-mile radius of East Chester I stayed quiet, lest I'd stir up trouble for myself. Ma's hands were gripped so tight to the steering wheel I'd probably have to pry her fingers loose once we got home. When we finally pulled up to the maternity home, Margaret jumped out of the car. An old grey suitcase was sitting at the end of the driveway.

"Hey, that's mine," she squawked, slamming the car door shut. She made for Ma to roll down her window. "Thanks for the ride," she said as she picked up her suitcase and started walking toward the maternity home.

"Do you think she'll last?" I asked as we headed down the road.

"Not likely," said Ma, stepping on the gas.

I didn't plan to spend my time worrying about Margaret. Ma was right. Mrs. Young wasn't likely to put up with her for long. Looking down at the thick envelope in my hands, I gave it a squeeze. I was anxious to get home and see what new pictures Aunt Maggie had sent.

"What the devil's going on there?" said Ma as she applied the brakes. I looked up just as she stopped the car. There seemed to be some kind of scuffle going on by the road leading down to the dump, but I didn't see what Ma thought she could do about it. Opening the car door, she removed the umbrella she kept in the back seat for rainy days.

"Ma, you don't even know who it is," I said. It made no sense to get mixed up in a stranger's brawl.

She looked at me and, in a serious tone, ordered me to stay in the car. "Do you hear, Tulia May? Don't you come near."

# Chapter Twenty-One

Ma marched up the road with a look of determination as she held tight to the umbrella. I sat at the edge of my seat holding my breath. Cranking down the window a bit, I stuck my head out to hear. If those boys knew what was good for them they'd run off before she got there. Ma was small but mighty and not to be underestimated. The day two of my nephews got into a squabble out near the barn, Ma was quick to put them in their place. She grabbed each one by the ear and twisted until they were both on their knees crying uncle. What a sight they made—both of them big strapping boys and Ma just a little over five feet. There was never a cross word between them again when they come to visit.

I sat spellbound as fists continued to fly. The boys were so absorbed in battle they didn't see Ma closing in on them. It didn't take a genius to figure out that whoever was on the bottom was in deep trouble. I flinched as

Ma brought her umbrella down across the boys' heads and backs, demanding they break it up this instant. Squawking, they put their arms up over their heads to protect themselves from the blow of the umbrella. She was beating hard and furious with no signs of letting up. I hoped she wouldn't get knocked over in the tussle, but she was faster than I would have thought and kept back far enough to avoid being kicked. Dust rolled into the air. For a moment I wanted to laugh, Ma getting the best of two boys nearly twice her size. When they finally separated and scrambled to their feet, I gasped. It was Guy and Kevin. I sat up closer to the windshield of the car, trying to see who was lying on the ground. Knowing Kevin and Guy, they could have been beating up anyone, but I couldn't stop the strange feeling that was wrapping itself around me.

"Get away from me, you crazy lady," Kevin cried as he backed away from Ma. He looked surprised to see who had attacked him. I'm sure he'd never witnessed such a sight in all his days—someone Ma's size and age fearlessly standing up to him.

"You want crazy? I'll show you crazy," she shouted. She came at the both of them again with the umbrella high above her head. She was about as riled up as I'd ever seen.

They didn't stick around for more punishment. They tore off down the road to the dump before the umbrella made contact again, their feet digging into the gravel.

"I'll be reporting this to your mother, Guy! Don't think I won't!" Ma hollered after them—a threat I knew she meant to carry through with. Guy's mother belonged to the Women's Institute, which meant Ma saw her on a regular basis. Ma wasn't one to put up with such shenanigans, especially from any of the neighbourhood kids. She'd make sure Mrs. Leary heard all about it. I'd seen Mrs. Leary blasting Guy before. I wouldn't want to be him when his mother found out.

I hung back in the car as Ma bent over the person on the ground. Whoever it was, he wasn't moving. I didn't wait for Ma to tell me that I could get out. I jumped out of the car and ran toward them. A deep sense of dread was gnawing away at me the closer I came.

"Finny Paul!" I cried out. Fear stopped me in my tracks. If Guy and Kevin had beat Finny senseless, I didn't want to see. I waited for a split second, then saw him move. Relief filled my lungs and I pulled in a gulp of air. I heard him groan and I rushed to help him up from the dirt.

"You're bleeding!" I shrieked. There was a small cut below his right eye and a steady stream of blood was dripping from his bottom lip. Grabbing hold of his arm, I attempted to haul him up. He pulled back, refusing my help.

"I'm okay," he said as he shuffled to his feet on his own power. This was no time for him to be exerting his independence. Everyone needs help from time to time. Finny was acting as if he was above all that. He brushed away the dirt that was biting at his palms and then removed the dust and gravel from his jeans.

"I expect you'll live," Ma said without an ounce of sympathy.

"I knew this was going to happen, Finny. I just knew it. You've got to steer clear of those two hooligans. They beat up Eric Conrad last month and now you. I hate them."

"Tulia," Ma scolded, the same way she did whenever I used that word. Ma didn't believe in hate. *It's what's wrong with the world*, she used to say.

"Oh Ma, it's true. They make fun of everyone. Ever since Kevin moved to East Chester, Guy's been nothing but a bully."

"That may be so, but hate's not the answer. That's why we're in the middle of a war—here," she said, pulling a handkerchief from her dress pocket and handing it to Finny. He hesitated before taking it. I thought, *Don't you be too proud, Finny Paul. It's a little late for that.*

"Thanks for your help, Mrs. Thompson," Finny mumbled, dabbing at the corner of his mouth with the handkerchief. He sounded embarrassed.

"Yes, well, two against one is a coward's fight," she said, her nose slightly turned upward.

Seeing that Finny was doing a poor job of cleaning the blood from his face, I took the handkerchief from him. "Let me," I said, lightly patting the cut below his eye. I stopped the trickle of blood that was creeping across his cheek. "You're going to have a shiner out of this racket," I said, although I figured he knew as much. He winced slightly, even though I was being as gentle as I could.

Ma picked her umbrella up out of the dirt and waved us on. "Now into the car with you," she said. "I'm driving you home."

It took a moment for me to realize that she was talking to Finny. I about fell over from shock. The last thing I thought I'd ever see was Ma driving out to Evy Paul's house.

Finny looked as though he was thinking the same. "I'm fine, Mrs. Thompson, really. I can get home on my own."

"Of course you can get home on your own, but that's not the point. I won't have you arguing with me, Finny Paul. Now get into the car at once."

I glanced back at Finny as we headed out to the Paul farm. He was slumped down in the seat, still holding the handkerchief to his mouth. Every now and then he'd look at it to see if he was still bleeding.

Evy stood out on the doorstep as Ma came up the driveway. The wind was blowing strands of red hair around her face. Mrs. James told me that back when Evy and Bobby were dating, Evy and Ma got along famously.

"Just like mother and daughter. To tell the truth, I think the breakup was harder on your mother than it was on Bobby. Two whole months," Mrs. James added.

"Your mother mourned for two whole months when Evy broke it off."

"Stay here," Ma ordered Finny when the car came to a stop. She got out and walked toward the house. There was a look of concern on Evy's face. I thought no wonder my brother Bobby wanted to marry her. She was the prettiest mother in East Chester, and I was sure she didn't even know it.

"I wonder what she's saying," Finny said.

I didn't tell him, but I was thinking the same thing. Ma finally motioned for Finny to get out of the car and Evy ran toward him.

"Look at you, Finny," she said. "Just look at you."

"That was nice, Ma—what you did for Finny today," I said that evening as we sat knitting socks for the soldiers.

"It was nothing more than anyone else would have done," she said, glancing up from her stitches. But we both knew that wasn't right.

"Oh Ma, can't you just for once say thank you when you get a compliment?" To be honest, Ma's actions today were a little confusing. Just when I thought she wouldn't do a thing nice for Finny Paul, she goes and saves his hide. I started to laugh as I thought about those boys running away from Ma like that, scared like little kids.

"What are you laughing about?" said Ma with a bemused look on her face.

"Oh nothing," I said, knitting a stitch. For a time there was nothing but the soft sound of our needles clicking together, and then, smiling, Ma said, "I guess they weren't such big men after all."

# Chapter Twenty-Two

"Be careful, Ma," I cried, pulling back seconds before a stickpin grazed my neck.

"Stop wiggling," she mumbled through a mouthful of pins. She looked like Finny's dog the time he tangoed with the porcupine and had quills sticking out of him everywhere. Pulling a pin out from between her pursed lips, she tacked the last bit of the lace to the neckline of my dress. She removed the extra pins from her mouth and set them on the edge of her sewing table. As much sewing as she did, she never found use for a pin cushion.

"It's nice to see you changed your mind about the dance," she said, leaning back in her chair. "I thought you'd come around." She was smiling because she thought she'd won. She had no idea the real reason behind my change of heart was seeing Beecher Merry. Ma being at the dance was sure to put a damper on things, but I vowed to remain positive. What's the point in going to a dance if you're not going to dance? She couldn't watch me the entire time.

I looked at my reflection in the full-length mirror. I couldn't help but admire Ma's handiwork. There wasn't anything she couldn't sew when she set her mind to it. She'd found a dress at the bottom of an old trunk. It was one she'd made for my oldest sister, Vera, a long time ago. The green cotton material still looked like new. The dress was too big for me the way it was, so she took all the pieces apart and cut them to fit me. She even changed the style and made it like the one I saw in the spring catalogue. When she put all those pieces together it didn't resemble the dress she started with at all.

I turned slightly to see the back. It flared out perfectly when I spun around. I could hardly wait to get out on the dance floor. If only Ma wouldn't be hovering around me like a hen hawk all night long. I'd been secretly hoping, praying even, that Beecher would make it to the dance. Other than a chance to visit Quintland, it was the only thing I dreamed of. Ma wouldn't approve of my dancing with him. Him being Jim Merry's son, I figured she'd be doubly against it. The less I knew about Becky's baby the better. She'd probably think I was trying to get information about him or something silly like that.

"Now take it off," she ordered as I continued to admire my reflection. I turned toward her, pulling my hair up out of the way so that she could help me with the zipper. It took some doing to convince her to put one in until I pointed out that people would take notice if she kept up with the latest trends.

"There's nothing wrong with buttons," I'd said with a slyness that Ma didn't even see coming, "but most of the dresses in the catalogue have zippers in them now." I pushed my luck and asked for broad shoulders like the kind Greta Garbo wore.

"What goes on in Hollywood is make-believe. We live in the real world, not some fairy tale conjured up for the movies." Ma was never influenced by what the starlets were wearing. I knew it was a long shot but I figured why not. *The squeaky wheel gets the grease*—Ma's words, not mine. Too bad that never worked on Ma when I was the one doing the squeaking.

"Can I get a pair of silk hose for the dance? Hope and some of the other girls are going to."

"And waste fifty cents? I can imagine their parents will have something to say about that. Girls get silly notions in their heads. Silk stockings," she clucked as she dropped the pins into the little mustard tin she kept them in.

"Come on, Ma, can't you give in just this once? What's it going to hurt? I've got my stipend money from Mrs. Young."

"And it's not to be wasted on foolishness."

"It's not like I asked to wear lipstick or pressed powder.

It's just silk hose...I never get anything." Hope said that only little kids wore socks with a dress. Not that I cared what other people would think, but I wanted to look good in case Beecher *did* show up.

"Never thought I'd see you acting the fool like all those girls you were so quick to criticize in the past," said Ma.

"And I never thought you wouldn't care what I looked like in public." I grunted my displeasure. I should have known better than to ask.

"Your regular socks will do fine," she said. I rolled my eyes. Apparently "best dressed" didn't include silk stockings as far as Ma was concerned.

Ma carefully pulled the dress up over my head, leaving me standing there in my underwear. I quickly dressed back into my clothes. I should consider myself lucky that Ma agreed to put in a zipper without pushing for anything else. I'd still be the envy of all the girls at the dance, since many of them would be wearing their sisters' hand-me-downs. I hoped at least Beecher noticed.

"Now hurry along and get those diapers and gowns into the car. I want to stitch the lace on your dress before we leave." Ma's feet had already found the rhythm as the sewing machine clacked away. I loaded all that would fit into a laundry basket just as Ma cut the last thread on my dress. Hemming would come later. She'd wash and iron it before the dance, press the pleats and starch the lace. It would be perfect, or as near perfect as possible.

"I'll bring the rest of the diapers when I come," she said, gathering up another load. I'd no more than set the basket into the back of the car when I heard the crash from inside the house, followed by a loud, mournful cry from Ma.

"Ma!" I cried, hushing into the house. She was lying on the floor at the bottom of the stairs, gowns and diapers slung helter-skelter. Reaching the bottom of the stairs, I stopped abruptly. She wasn't moving. Holding my hand in front of her mouth and nose, I tried to determine if she was still breathing. Just then her eyes snapped open.

I'm not sure which one of us gasped the loudest.

# Chapter Twenty-Three

❧ *888* ❧

"I brought your sewing, Mrs. Young," I said with a basket of flannelette diapers—all I could carry—looped over my arm. "There's more at the house. Ma sprained her ankle real bad and Doctor Rafuse says it's the worst he's ever seen. She's got to stay off it for at least four weeks."

"Your poor mother—is she all right?" There was a genuine sound of concern in Mrs. Young's voice as she took the basket of diapers from my arms.

"As right as anyone with a sprained ankle could be," I said. She was propped up on a chair in the parlour when I left the house; her knitting needles were going a mile a minute. A look of pain crossed her face, but she was too stubborn to admit it. The Women's Institute gave out a bunch of sock yarn at their last meeting, so she'd at least have something to keep her busy while she was laid up.

"But of course," said Mrs. Young. "What was I thinking?

Get into the car. I'll come out for the rest."

I should have known that her charitable offer had nothing to do with making things easier for me. When she left our house that day with the rest of the diapers and gowns, she'd talked Ma into having me help out at the home every day after school. It was hardly something I could object to, since I knew we couldn't go four weeks without any money coming in. On the brighter side, I'd be able to visit the nursery more often and I wouldn't have to listen to Ma's complaints about not being able to do anything around the house.

"I wouldn't ask, but we're short-staffed, and now with you out of commission, Naomi." Mrs. Young shook her head and gave a pitiful look. "It would be just until you're back on your feet. It would be a tremendous help to me."

Ma never did seem able to say no to Mrs. Young.

—

"I'll take some cream in my tea when you get around to it, Tulia," Ma called from the living room. I closed my eyes.

*One...two...three....* I'd heard somewhere that counting to ten when you're at your wits' end was a good way to keep from blowing your stack. This was the third time she'd asked me to get her something that morning. Didn't she care that I was trying to get ready for school? Ma being unable to do anything more than hobble around a little didn't stop her from bossing everyone in her path.

It was driving me up the wall. Whenever I complained that she was being too demanding, she'd remind me of the constant pain she was in.

Doctor Rafuse gave strict orders for her to stay off that ankle of hers, and "No cheating," he added, wagging his finger at the end of his speech. He knew Ma wasn't one for sitting back and letting others do the work for her. I watched her last evening, attempting to stand using the crutches Becky had borrowed from the hospital for her. I was ready to holler, but she made some faces and quickly sat back down. It would be awhile before she was ready for crutches, which only meant more waiting on her for me and Becky.

"Becky'll get your tea, Ma. I'm running late." I pushed myself to sound cheery, but I was dreading the thought that Becky was soon leaving. I'd be left to deal with Ma on my own. I grabbed my schoolbooks and hurried toward the door, at the same time sending Becky a sly grin.

"Thanks a lot, Tulia," she said, playfully throwing a balled-up tea towel in my direction. I ducked and headed for the front door.

"I'll see you after work, Ma." As I reached the front door Ma called out for Becky to get her tea.

"Hold your horses, Ma. I've only got two hands."

I closed the door behind me and smiled. It was fun having Becky back home. By the way she and Ma were behaving, no one would ever guess that anything had happened last year. It was just like old times again. Maybe Becky was right; maybe starting over was for the best.

I knew Ma didn't like having Becky taking time off work to be with her, but Becky insisted. While Becky had as much compassion as the next person, maybe more, her being a nurse, she had little patience when it came to dealing with Ma's constant list of demands. I couldn't much blame her. Hands down, Ma was *the* worse patient on the face of the earth. Since Becky could only get a few days off from her job, I wouldn't get a break for long. She was going to stay until after the weekend and then *she'll be all yours*—Becky's words, not mine. She was heading off to Halifax next month to enlist in the army. She'd warned Ma not to try and talk her out of it and, for a wonder, Ma was keeping quiet. I guess she knew Becky wouldn't change her mind anyway. I wasn't sure I was ready to deal with Ma on my own. Thank goodness Mrs. Story offered to help out during the day.

"I can fix your meals and we can visit," she said, but I think we all knew Ma would demand a little more than that. Truthfully, I think it made Mrs. Story feel helpful.

I went directly to the maternity home after school. Before heading to the laundry room, I snuck upstairs to the nursery. Babies were wailing and crying. Sally was attempting to change a dirty diaper while holding a baby in her arms. Another girl was walking the floor with a baby in each arm. I took the baby from Sally. She smiled and quickly pinned the diaper in place.

"I can't stay long," I said, handing the baby back to Sally. I hurried toward the crib by the window. It was empty.

"Where is she? Where's Cammie?" I said, near-panic spreading through me. Had someone adopted her? I didn't even get to say goodbye.

"It's okay, Tulia. Margaret just stepped out for a bottle. She took the baby with her."

"Margaret?" Surely Sally didn't mean the woman we had dropped off at the home the other week.

"Here she is," said Sally. I cringed. Ma said she wouldn't last, that Mrs. Young would send her on her way in no time. But there she was, and she was holding a baby—my baby—in her arms.

"Hey, I know you," said Margaret.

"I've got to do laundry," I said as I hurried from the nursery. I didn't trust what might come out of Margaret's mouth.

I made it to the laundry room only to find things in disarray. There was a dirty pail of diapers soaking that hadn't been washed. Water that had been spilled on the floor needed to be mopped up. Ma would have had all the diapers washed if she had been there, and she'd have made sure no one spilled water over the floor.

I scrubbed diapers on the scrub board the way Ma taught me and then I put them in the washing machine for another go around. I brought the rest of the dried clothes in from the line and folded them. There was a pile of newly washed sheets and gowns that needed ironing, but that would be a job for someone tomorrow. I put the clothes through the wringer and cleaned the washing machine. Next I went to work scrubbing the floor. Before I could dump the dirty water outside, someone knocked at the door.

"I was going by and saw you coming in from the clothesline," said Finny when I opened the door. The bruise under his eye had changed from black to green. The cut on his face had scabbed over. He hadn't been back to school since he got beat up. I wondered if he was ashamed to have people see him.

"Here...it's cleaned," he said, holding out the handkerchief Ma had given him last week.

"You didn't have to give it back," I said, knowing that Ma didn't expect it. I took the handkerchief and asked how things were going. He said fine but I could tell he wasn't being honest. I'd known Finny long enough to tell when something was troubling him. I'd heard that Mrs. Leary had marched Guy out to the Paul farm and made him apologize to Finny. She also made him promise it would never happen again. Someone at school said he'd been banned from spending time with Kevin.

"Wait a minute. I'm just about finished," I said when he turned to leave. "I'll walk with you." He looked like he needed someone to talk to. Finny didn't ask for a whole lot from our friendship. Seemed like he was the one always doing for me. I quickly dumped out the scrub water, then closed the door behind me. "So what's wrong?" I finally said as we walked down the road toward home.

"I'm joining up, Tulia," he said.

I stopped in the road and pulled on his arm until I was looking him in the face. "What do you mean, joining up?" He wasn't making any sense.

"I'm taking the bus into Halifax in a couple of weeks. I'm joining the army."

*A couple of weeks?* "Finny you're not old enough. You're not even fifteen."

"Will be in a few months." Finny was pulling my leg, he had to be.

We bickered back and forth for a time. For every reason I had for why he couldn't join the army, Finny came up with a reason why he could.

"Get real. Your parents aren't going let you join up," I finally said.

"Who says they're going to know?"

"You can't just run off—I'll tell." I could see that my words hit home and I thought I'd put an end to his foolish talk.

"No you won't, Tulia." Finny said with far too much confidence. There was no way Finny was going to try and join the army if I had any say in the matter.

"How do you know that?" I boldly challenged. Looking

me straight in the eye, he didn't flinch.

"Because I'm never telling *your* secret."

——

"Yes, Ma, I cleaned up the laundry room before I left. There were diapers that needed washing, but Mrs. Young told me not to hang them out, that someone would do that in the morning."

"I doubted they'd get them all done," she said, sounding slightly pleased.

I gathered my knitting from the basket. "No one works as hard as you, Ma," I said, plunking myself down in the armchair. It had been a long day and I was tired. Becky was in the kitchen finishing up the last of the dishes. I secretly thought she was dawdling, trying to catch a break from Ma. Ma hadn't stopped questioning me since I got home. It was killing her not to be working out at the maternity home. For sure no one would do it to her satisfaction.

"Oh, I almost forgot, that woman's still there—that Margaret person we took out to the home," I said, starting a new row of knitting. Ma's knitting needles came to a sudden stop. She shook her head.

"Glory day. I suspect Mrs. Young will soon get her fill of that one." She resumed her knitting. I could only hope Ma was right.

# Chapter Twenty-Four

*very day, before heading into the laundry room, I'd sneak off to the nursery to see Cammie. And every day, I'd walk in to find Margaret hogging her for herself. I couldn't demand she hand the baby over—as if that would even work. Sometimes she was giving her a bottle, other times she was rocking her. I hadn't been able to hold her all week long. Why wouldn't she leave her be? I thought now that I was working at the home every day I'd get more time with her. I said as much to Sally one day.

"Oh Tulia, that baby can use as much as love as she can get. Margaret's doing her a favour."

But then Monday came and Margaret wasn't in the nursery. A small splinter of glee pierced me. Maybe Ma was right, maybe Mrs. Young finally had her fill. With luck, I'd never see her again. Beneath the sound of babies crying, I could hear the rattling cough of a little one as I entered the nursery. The smell of baby poop was stronger than usual. I curled up my nose and rushed over to Cammie's crib. She was awake so I picked her up. I hugged her to me and rocked her in my arms. She fussed a little but quickly quieted. I made some silly faces but she didn't smile at me the way she usually did.

"Is she sick?" I asked a girl who was rocking a crying baby. I knew how quickly colds could spread in a nursery full of babies.

"Who's to say? I just feed them and change their diapers when I'm told to. One more week of this misery and my bill will be paid off. I'll be long gone from here."

I looked around at the babies in the cribs. Some were on the floor crawling around, reaching for crib rungs and pulling at sheets. It was a most pitiful sight, all those babies and most of them being ignored. I wondered how often Mrs. Young came to the nursery to check on them and just what she would do if one of them got sick. I kissed Cammie's head and laid her back down. Mrs. Young's car was in the driveway, which meant she was home. She'd expect me to be doing my chores.

I started down the stairs to the laundry room. About halfways down, I stopped short when I saw who was down there working. *Margaret!* I wanted to scream. She was a sad-looking sight with her sleeves rolled up like she meant business. Her hair, although tied behind her, had come loose and much of it was dangling in her face.

"What are *you* doing down *here*?" I said above the churning of the washing machines.

"Well, well, well…if it's not the little scarf thief."

I should have known she was just waiting for her chance to bring that up. Anger jabbed at me.

"I didn't steal anything," I barked as I reached the bottom of the stairs. "No one in their right mind would jump off a bus and go chasing after a stupid scarf."

Margaret's expression quickly softened and she smiled. "Lighten up, kid—I was just having a little fun with you. No need to get your drawers in a knot."

"You had no right accusing me that day," I snapped.

"I got my scarf back, though—didn't I?"

"'Please' would have worked too." And just the way I said it struck me funny in that moment. I let out a nervous snigger that turned into a full-out belly laugh and pretty soon she was laughing along with me. I had to admit it did seem kind of funny now.

"That old battleaxe sent me down here this morning," she said once our laughter died down. "Said I was better suited for work in the laundry. She didn't want me hanging around the nursery is all, seeing all the things that weren't right. Anyway, I'm some glad you showed up. I've been slaving away down here all day. She sent down a few girls to help but most of them are useless—rich girls who wouldn't know their head from a hole in the ground. Please tell me *you* know what you're doing," she added.

I had to admit, the laundry room looked fairly neat, almost as good as when Ma was here. Water wasn't slopped over the floor and there were no pails of dirty diapers waiting to be washed. The last load of laundry was sloshing back and forth and Margaret was working her way through a stack of diapers that needed ironing.

"Ma works here most days, but she sprained her ankle real bad. That's why she's not here. I help her sometimes." I chided myself for blurting out our business like that. I hardly knew a thing about this woman, but then I figured, what's the harm? Everyone in East Chester knew Ma worked at the maternity home. It wasn't a secret.

I went about my work and said very little the rest of the afternoon—I didn't need to. Margaret talked almost non-stop, like she was starved for conversation. Some of the most incredible subjects flowed from her mouth, everything from her theory on what all was wrong with the world to some of the popular songs that were being played on the radio. She told me about her feeble granny who brought both her and her sister up and how she'd inherited her old house when she died.

"Not that I was anxious to stay in Tanner, mind you—it's so small you can't leave town without meeting yourself coming back. Brenda's the one who was going to go off and make her mark in the world," she said, putting her attention into her ironing. "But then she found herself in the family way and all that changed." The mention of Tanner got my interest.

"What's wrong?" she said when she saw I'd suddenly stopped putting clothes through the wringer. Reaching into the washer, I shook my head. I had no intentions of mentioning Beecher Merry to her, even though it seemed an odd coincidence, her living in Tanner. What were the chances?

She talked about her sister that afternoon and how no one here at the home seemed to know who she was. "They act like she was invisible. You'd think someone would remember her."

"Most people aren't here very long." I didn't know what else to say. The girls were warned not to talk about anything, or anyone, when they came to the home. I'd overheard Mrs. Young say so myself.

"You know what I think?" she said suddenly. Whatever it was, I was sure she wasn't about to keep it to herself. "I think that baby in the nursery is Brenda's. You know, the little one with the blonde hair. She was supposed to have been adopted, but Mrs. Young says whatever she likes. She's the spitting image of Brenda—the baby, that is." It made sense now, all the attention she gave Cammie.

"I tried looking through Mrs. Young's files the other day but I couldn't find anything with Brenda's name on it."

"You went through her files?" Talk about brazen, snooping through Mrs. Young's papers like that. "Weren't you scared of getting caught?" The adoptions were all private. Mrs. Young took those matters most seriously. I didn't even want to think about what she'd do if she caught someone going through her paperwork.

Margaret shrugged. "What's she going to do, kick me out? Tell me to pack my bags and go? I've got nothing to lose." I wasn't sure if she should be admired for her spunk or if she was downright crazy for taking such a chance.

"She gives them all new names when they come here," I said, shaking out the clothes I'd just put through the wringer. It seemed only fair to tell her, and it might keep her from further snooping.

"Great," she said, throwing her hands into the air. "So there's no way to find out and I can't ask the old battleaxe." She paused. "But you know, the more I think about it, the more I'm sure she's Brenda's." She was staring off in the distance as if thinking of something, then suddenly snapped out of it. She looked at me and sighed. "Anyway, that's my problem, not yours. Look at that—they're all done," she said setting the iron down.

On the way home I could hardly wait to tell Ma about my day. She'd be interested to hear that Margaret had been moved down to the laundry. We'd have a good laugh when I told her all the things Margaret had gone on about, all the troubles in the world and life with her ailing granny. But as my feet hit the front steps, my enthusiasm slowed.

"You can heat up the stew Mrs. Story made yesterday."

Ma looked up from her knitting when I entered the parlour. "How did things go at work today?" I looked at the pair of socks on the chair beside Ma—her effort for the day. It would be another two weeks before she'd be back in the laundry room. That meant another two weeks of my working alongside Margaret. If I told Ma that Mrs. Young had put her in the laundry to work, she could probably get Mrs. Young to send her someplace else. There was still the kitchen. Margaret would be out of my hair. I wouldn't have to listen to her chatter.

"Things went fine, Ma," I said, heading off to the kitchen to heat our stew. "Things went just fine."

# Chapter Twenty-Five

"Bout Mrs. Young, please, I changed my mind. I don't want to give him up."

I stopped suddenly, recognizing Sally's voice coming from Mrs. Young's office. I'd learned from Margaret that Sally would soon be going home. Pulling in a deep breath, I moved in closer to hear. The door was slightly ajar. Sally was wearing a hat and coat like she was ready to go somewhere. She was hanging on to Mrs. Young's arm, pulling at her almost, and Mrs. Young was standing all stiff and proper without a pinch of sympathy on her face.

"You're far too emotional to be making such a life-altering decision, Sally. It's why you signed a contract when you first came here, when your thinking was clearer."

"Mrs. Young, please," she said through a sea of tears.

"I'm afraid the contract is legal and binding. I couldn't go back on it if I wanted to."

"But I want to take him home," she gulped.

"Your parents didn't pay good money to keep your secret only to have you show up with an illegitimate baby."

"Can't I at least see him?"

"Your baby has been placed with a loving family. He's gone and that's all that's to it." At that point, Sally began to all-out wail and my heart made a wild lurch.

"Now pull yourself together. You've been given a fresh new start. Not everyone in your situation is as fortunate. You'll have more children when the time is right."

"I hate you," cried Sally, now sobbing uncontrollably. She turned quickly and rushed out of the room. The door nearly hit me and I jumped back. She stopped short when she saw me but then hurried away, sobbing. Mrs. Young looked out at me. Her eyes were hard and unyielding. I stepped back, preparing for a scolding. I had no right listening in. Ma would have a conniption if she found out.

"Please close the door, Tulia," she said quietly. I stood half-stunned. Anyone with half a heart would have felt sorry for Sally, but not Mrs. Young. She didn't look the least bit upset. When she saw that I hadn't moved, she finally said, "Shouldn't you be helping Margaret in the laundry?"

"You're late. What took you so long?" Margaret was peeking out the door when I came down the stairs. On my way to the laundry I'd decided not to tell her what I'd overheard. I'd have to listen to her ranting about Mrs. Young the rest of the afternoon if I did.

"Come here," she said, motioning for me to come close. I couldn't imagine what she was up to. "Sally's taking the bus home today. It'll soon be pulling up." Grabbing me by the hand, she opened the door and yanked me outside. Sally was waiting at the end of the driveway, holding fast to her suitcase.

"Hurry," Margaret said and we ran, hand-in-hand, full speed across the grass. I looked back toward the maternity home. If Mrs. Young was still in her office she might see us. I could hear the rumbling of the bus in the distance. I kept running. Some things are too important to let worry stand in your way.

"Sally...Sally—wait up!" Margaret called out, waving her hand in the air as we reached the gravel stones in the driveway. Sally turned and, seeing us, dropped her suitcase. She hugged first Margaret and then me. I held back tears. Sally had been at the home for months. The nursery wouldn't be the same without her. Even Margaret was swatting away tears.

"You take care of yourself," she said to Sally as the bus pulled up. Sally straightened her shoulders back. She gathered her suitcase and stepped onto the bus in a dignified manner. I didn't imagine I'd ever see her again. She looked at us through the bus window and held up her hand to wave. I thought about that day in town when she'd mistakenly got off the bus, how lost and scared she'd looked. The bus drove off and I saw that she had that same look now.

"Let's get back before the old battleaxe catches us out here," said Margaret with a sniff.

With the laundry room cleaned for the day, I was anxious to go home. Ma was supposed to have my dress hemmed for the dance and I wanted to try it on one last time. I could hardly believe she'd agreed to let me go with Marlee and Hope, even with Marlee's parents going along. Maybe being laid up was softening her a bit. They say whenever God closes a door, he most always opens a window somewhere. I couldn't help seeing the silver lining in Ma's sprained ankle. She'd been difficult to get along with, that was true, but at least she wouldn't be hovering over me at the dance.

"I've made up my mind, kid. I'm leaving here," said Margaret just as I gathered my things to go.

"You can't leave—what about your sister's bill?" I couldn't believe it—first Sally and now Margaret. I was getting used to her being around. She made me laugh sometimes. In the beginning I didn't think it would be possible, but I enjoyed working with her.

"Oh that," she scoffed, waving her hand. "Mrs. Young's

not going to miss that little bit—not with all the money she's raking in."

"But your job...Mrs. Young...." Which amounted to me saying that I didn't want her to go, that I liked—yes, liked—having her around. And Ma wouldn't be back to work for two more weeks.

"Look, kid, I only came here to find out about Brenda and her baby. I hit a brick wall and there's nothing else I can do. You can't squeeze blood from a turnip."

"But the baby. You said she might be your sister's." She'd never see her again. Surely she wouldn't just walk away.

"That's the thing. I've been thinking on that a lot. That's why I'm taking her with me."

I was confused. "You're adopting her?"

"Adopt-shmopt—why should I have to pay for my own sister's baby? That old battleaxe's not just going to give her to me. She'll try to make me pay."

"But if you're *not* adopting her?" Margaret gave me a sheepish look, and then it started to make sense. "You mean you're...." I was in disbelief.

"Don't look so shocked, kid. You can't always sit back and do nothing. The baby can't stay here."

"Cammie!" I barked. "Her name is Cammie. You can't just call her 'the baby.' She's got a name."

"Okay then—Cammie." Margaret didn't look as if she cared one way or another about her name.

I started shaking my head. "No! You can't have her.

I won't let you." What Margaret was talking about—it wasn't right. "I'll tell Mrs. Young what you're planning."

There was no way I'd let her steal Cammie away. This was her home, here with me. Margaret was practically a stranger.

"Then that baby's as good as dead. Is that what you want? Do you want Cammie to die?" she said, staring me in the eye.

"No, you're just saying that." The words thumped against my eardrums as I spoke. People will say anything to get their own way. I'd heard Margaret tell some pretty wild stories. Maybe she was making all that up.

"Grow up and see things the way they are. She's nothing but skin and bones now. She can hardly hold her head up. Every week it's a little worse. I've been sneaking her bottles at night but she doesn't always take them."

"Sneaking bottles?"

"Well, she can't live on molasses and water." Margaret turned her head toward the ceiling. "'That baby's not going to live.' That's what she said yesterday—'That baby's not going to live,' like she didn't even care. Well, I care. Any nitwit would have to care."

"Mrs. Young wouldn't...she just wouldn't." My head was spinning. None of what Margaret was saying could be true. It just couldn't be. And yet something niggled at me, a feeling I couldn't shake, a thought dark and sinister.

"How many babies do you think die out here? They're

not all stillborn, I can tell you that. Cammie's got to go—that's all that's to it. Now, I've been coming up with some plans, but I can't do it all on my own. I saw Jim Merry in town a few weeks back. You know him?"

I nodded. "He brings lumber out sometimes."

The rest of what she said was a blur. I wasn't sure what she'd said to convince him to help her and I didn't much care. All the uneasiness I'd felt about the home came flooding over me—that morning in the cove when Finny and me saw old Joe dump something into the water and that little body in the butterbox, lying cold and frozen inside the shed. Finny was right. He'd been right all along. As much as I didn't want to believe it, deep down inside I knew these things were true. I struggled to keep from crying. Crying wouldn't change a thing. And then I was aware of Margaret shaking me. I looked up.

"I said, there's a dance on Saturday—are you listening?" I nodded.

I was now.

# Chapter Twenty-Six

⌒*888*⌐

"Julia May, will you stop strutting in front of the mirror like a peacock? Your ride's here."

Sometimes it felt as though Ma knew me a little too well. I took one last look at myself. Last night I'd fussed over the bobby pins Ma put in my hair. It now seemed worth the discomfort I'd felt sleeping in them overnight. The curls were lying perfectly against my head. Ma did her best to hide a smile when she pinned her good tortoiseshell clip in my hair. But I could tell she was pleased. From the top of my head to the tips of my toes, everything felt perfect, even without the stockings I'd wanted.

I touched the locket Aunt Maggie had given me last summer. I'd replaced the picture of the quints with one of Becky in her nurse's uniform to keep her near. Ma seemed proud that Becky had signed up and would be helping patch up the injured troops overseas. Knowing

Ma, it could have been an act, her trying to be brave for my sake. She said we should try not to think about the danger Becky might be in.

"We'll write and send care packages and when the war's over we'll be waiting." She made it sound simple. I couldn't help thinking about Uncle Oscar and the candles she'd lit for him during the last war.

"Did you hear me, Tulia? I said your ride's here."

"Yes, Ma, I heard." I raced down the steps before Ma yelled again. She was waiting for me by the door. A few days back, Doctor Rafuse had given her the okay to start walking a little without the crutches. The bruising had changed from blue to green to yellow. If all went well, she'd be back working in the laundry sometime next week.

"I'll wait up," Ma said, straightening my dress collar. "Now behave yourself and stay out of trouble." I could still hardly believe she was allowing me to go without being there to watch over me. Marlee's mother must have said all the right things, and it probably didn't hurt none that Mr. Fuller gave his word that he'd have me home by ten-thirty, which Ma said was plenty late for me to be out.

"And Tulia?" Ma practically whispered the words. "Have a good time." I gave her a quick hug before heading off. She laughed and playfully swatted at me. "Just get going," she said.

Guilt's tiny teeth nibbled at me as I hurried out the

door. *What you don't know won't hurt you*—Finny's words, not mine. I drew in a big breath and hoped Finny Paul was right as I squeezed in the back seat between Hope and Marlee.

People were dancing the foxtrot when we arrived, their graceful moves filling the dance floor.

"This is our dance," said Mr. Fuller, smiling at his wife. Wasting no time, he took Mrs. Fuller's hand and they moved onto the dance floor. They stepped with elegance, each footstep perfectly matched, and I thought it must be nice to have parents who were young and graceful. I'd only ever had Daddy and Ma, and if they'd ever danced together it was long before I was born. Maybe not at all.

"Let's get some juice," squealed Hope. She had on the dress her sister wore to the spring dance three years ago. She looked more grown-up than I'd ever seen. We told her she could pass for fifteen if she wanted to. Her braided hair was wrapped around her head, forming a neat bun at the top. Ma said I was too young to wear my hair up and that Mrs. Steward's leniency might one day be Hope's undoing. I didn't exactly know what that meant—only that I wouldn't be wearing my hair up anytime soon. Hope grabbed our hands and led us toward the refreshment table.

"Strawberry and grape," said Marlee, reaching for a cup that held red juice. I absently reached for one too, mostly to make myself look busy. The music was loud and the dance hall was quickly filling up. Butterflies stirred inside me as I checked around for Beecher. I took a sip of juice but couldn't taste it going down. I wasn't sure if I was more nervous about the dance or what was to come after.

"*We'll have a head start. No one will know we're gone until the morning, maybe later. By then it will be too late.*" I pushed Margaret's words out of my head. It was too late to be going over any of this now.

"Did you see who just arrived?" said Hope, using her most uppity-sounding voice. I knew she meant Catherine and her group of friends before I even looked. Catherine's hair was piled stylishly on top of her head and under the lights of the dance hall it was the reddest I'd ever seen it look. She was wearing a blue dress she'd worn before. There was no denying it looked good on her.

"Your dress is way nicer." Hope would be the one to notice. She always said that no one could change a sow's ear into a silk purse the way Ma could.

A burst of laughter erupted around Catherine and her friends. Heads in the dance hall turned toward the sound.

"Good grief," muttered Marlee, "How's anyone supposed to compete with her?"

"It's not as if she's been asked to dance," I pointed out. I silently wondered what could be keeping Beecher so long. Margaret had promised that Jim Merry was bringing him to the dance. It was all part of the plan.

"Come on," said Hope when she saw that some of the other girls had doubled up to dance. Marlee looked at Hope and shrugged. "Better than standing here doing nothing," she said. Grabbing each other's hands, they made their way onto the dance floor like they had for the past two years. They weren't the only girls dancing with their friends for lack of an invitation from a boy. Finny walked in with Trevor and once again I was jabbed by the reality of the evening ahead. I'd gone over the details with him several times. From the moment he heard about the plan, he was keen to help out. Finny always did choose the side of the underdog. It was why I'd asked for his help and, really, he was the only one I could trust with something this important.

I was going over the plan in my head one more time when the music suddenly stopped. Hope and Marlee came rushing over to where I was. As I looked across the room, I sucked in my breath. Beecher was standing off to the side, surveying the room, and our eyes met. A part of me had worried he might not come, that all the plans we'd made had been for nothing. I gave a nervous wave as relief quivered through me.

"That must be him," Marlee whispered. "Is that him, Tulia?" she asked, directing her question at me. My own apprehension prevented me from answering. I stood there with a smile fixed on my face. I feared there was a real danger that my jaws might stay permanently locked.

"We'd better give them some privacy," giggled Hope. They hurried onto the dance floor as the music started up again.

From there, much of the evening was a blur. Our sentences were awkward at first, neither of us used to making small talk. Slowly the words began to run smooth so that anyone listening in might have thought we had always known each other. I remember moving out onto the dance floor, although it was possible that I floated there. If we moved at all in time to the music I surely don't remember. There were sips of juice and silly jokes, none of which I can recall but by the amount of laughing I did they must have been funny. Apart from Finny Paul, Beecher was the only boy who'd ever said more than a sentence or two to me. I wasn't sure what the evening would mean in the long run, but for tonight I didn't care.

I introduced Beecher to Finny. "Finny will be driving Margaret out to meet your father," I explained without elaborating any further. I could have said we were going to steal my mother's car and that Finny wasn't old enough for a licence, and that Margaret really wasn't adopting the baby, but there seemed no sense in giving all those details.

The evening really couldn't have been more spectacular—that is, until Kevin and Guy swaggered into the dance hall. Seeing them together made me uneasy. They hadn't been hanging out since the two of them beat up Finny a month ago. I looked quickly about for Finny. This seemed like something he should know about. He'd been talking to Trevor and Hank earlier in the evening. He wasn't one for dancing. I was a bit surprised when he told me he was planning to come.

I waved to catch Finny's attention, to warn him to watch out for Guy and Kevin, but he slipped out the door before I could warn him. Ten o'clock—he was on his way to East Chester, the first step of our plan. Kevin and Guy shared a look and a quick nod as they made their way toward the exit. I had to warn Finny. There was no telling what would happen. Last time he'd been lucky; Ma happened along. What if Guy and Kevin ambushed him on his way to East Chester? Not only would Finny be in danger but our whole plan would be ruined.

I made my way across the dance floor, weaving in and around the couples. Beecher was behind me, telling me to slow down. But I couldn't slow down. There wasn't any time. I didn't stop to think about the right or wrong of my leaving the dance hall. I pushed Ma's warning to behave out of my head. Finny was one for saying that *sometimes you've got to act*. I knew then what he meant. If the evening needed saving, it was up to me to do something about it.

# Chapter Twenty-Seven

Clusters of stars dotted the sky above the dance hall, their lights not yet clearly visible. The air was pulsing with the high-pitched chirps of spring peepers. I had to find Finny. There were cars parked along both sides of the road for as far as I could see. Groups of people were standing around talking. There looked to be almost as many people outside the hall as there were inside. Some were smoking and drinking. From the open door, music from the Jack Banner Band snaked out into the night air. I searched around, desperate to find Finny.

"What's wrong, Tulia?" Beecher's brown eyes pleaded for an explanation as he grabbed my hand.

"I'm worried about Finny. Kevin and Guy—they'll beat him up again. There he is. Finny...wait up," I said, hurrying toward him.

"Tulia?" He sounded surprised as he waited for us to catch up.

"Kevin and Guy—"

"Hey, Indian boy!" The words reverberated into the night air. My heart jumped into my throat. The sound of feet scuffing across the gravel road grew louder. Within seconds, Kevin and Guy caught up to us.

"We were talking to you, Geronimo," said Kevin. I wanted to wipe the stupid smirk off his face. They were going to finish what they'd started last month. I'd never in my life wanted to punch someone before. For a second, time stood still and then anger exploded inside me. I starting screaming at Guy and Kevin to grow up, to leave Finny Paul alone. My palms thumped into Guy's chest and he was jarred backwards. Kevin started laughing, like he thought it was joke, and I turned toward him.

"You think it's funny?" I said, pushing him with all my force. My face was burning. "I'll tell you funny—two big guys who got beat up by an old woman with an umbrella—now that's funny." There was a shocked look on both of their faces. But no one was more surprised than me. Finny was to drive Margaret and Cammie to meet up with Jim Merry. There was no way that wasn't going to happen. Cammie needed to get away from that place. Kevin went to say something but I told him to shut his mouth. Then I pushed him. I pushed him so hard that he stumbled backward onto the ground. Within seconds he'd scrambled to his feet.

"You're crazy," he said, backing away. "You're crazy

just like your mother. Come on," he said to Guy. "Let's get out of here."

They raced off in the direction of the dance hall, the feet digging into the gravel. My legs trembled—my whole body trembled, stunned by my own actions. And then Finny and Beecher began to hoot and holler.

"I didn't know you were such a wildcat, Tulia," laughed Finny.

"No one's going to mess with you if they know what's good for them," agreed Beecher, equally amused. Suddenly, the anger that had been gripping me let go and I was laughing along with them. I had no idea where any of that came from or how I possessed the courage to stand up to Guy and Kevin. All I knew was that they deserved it and more.

"Is there some problem here?" I turned around and came face-to-face with Jim Merry, who seemed to have materialized from out of nowhere.

"No problem," I said, proud of myself for standing up to Guy and Kevin. "No problem at all."


I never realized how deadly quiet the nights in East Chester were, there never being a reason for me to be out and about at an outlandish hour. I thought how sounds seemed magnified tenfold as I snuck down the stairs and into the night. Finny was pacing the driveway and stopped when he saw me standing out on the front stoop. I was wearing a bandana and expected I looked quite different, but he didn't say anything if I did.

"Come on," I said, anxious to get going. We pushed the car down the driveway so that Ma wouldn't hear it start. Ordinarily she was a sound sleeper, but we couldn't take any chances. When Finny's first attempt to start the car failed, I asked him if he was sure he knew what he was doing.

"Do chickens have lips?" he said, going over the steps once more.

"No," I said without giving it a thought. *Of all the foolishness,* I thought.

"Yeah, well. I'm no chicken." I couldn't argue with him there, even though what he'd just said didn't make one iota of sense.

When the car finally started, he looked over at me and grinned.

"All ready?" he said, and I nodded.

"Ready as I'll ever be."

We couldn't do this without him. There was no way Margaret could carry Cammie all the way to Chester, lugging her old grey suitcase. Someone would be sure to see her on the road. It was also safe to say that there would be too much at stake if Jim came all the way out to the maternity home to pick her up. I pulled in a deep breath, confident with Finny beside me.

We headed toward Chester with Finny behind the wheel. I couldn't let myself think about what Ma would do if she ever found out. As we approached the maternity home, Finny slowed down. "Where's she going to be waiting?"

"Just up the road. By the big maple tree," I said, craning my neck for a clearer view. "There—there she is!"

Finny stopped the car and I jumped out. I opened the back door and tossed in Margaret's suitcase.

"What took so long?" she said, climbing into the back seat with Cammie in her arms. "I thought you weren't coming."

"I had to wait for Ma to fall asleep." I hadn't counted on Ma wanting to hear details about the dance. She even had a lunch set out for us when I got home.

*"Get ready for bed and come back down,"* she'd said. *"I want to hear all about it."*

The car bounced over potholes and bumps, but Finny didn't slow down.

"They can't be too far," he said as we rounded another bend.

"They'll go all night...to meet up with the freighters," said Margaret. "That's what Jim said." My concern was getting the car back into the driveway after we got Margaret and Cammie on the back of Jim Merry's wagon. From there, I would probably never know the rest.

"That's the wagon up ahead," said Finny, slowing down.

"Stay back," I warned. "If Jim sees me he might tell Ma."
A part of me felt like a fake not telling Beecher any of this.
But I couldn't risk it. The less Jim Merry knew about my
part in all this, the better. Finny took Margaret's suitcase
and approached the wagon. I could hear him talking to
Jim and Beecher, and the soft, gentle clang of ox bells.

"Thanks, kid...for everything," said Margaret. She
placed Cammie in my arms one last time. Cammie fussed
and I stroked her cheek the way she liked. She soon fell
back to sleep. Regret made my throat ache and I held back
tears. Why couldn't things have worked out differently?
Margaret was right. Mrs. Young was nothing but an old
battleaxe, her always making out she had everyone's best
interest at heart. What a joke. This whole thing was her
fault. If the maternity home got shut down, I didn't even
care. Ma and me would be all right. One way or another
we would.

"Take good care of her," I said, choking back tears.

"I'll do my best at least until Brenda comes back,"
Margaret said. "No need to worry, she'll be safe."

I kissed Cammie's cheek and handed her back to
Margaret. She looked at me as if she had something
more to say.

"Listen, kid, you should probably know my name's not
really Margaret. It's Millie—Millie Turple," she said, but
then I'd known that from the first day we met, the way
she stumbled over her name, like she didn't even know it

herself. "We won't be that far away. Maybe you can come out sometime...you know, to check on her."

"That sounds swell," I said, although I think we both knew that wasn't likely to happen.

"I'm coming," said Millie, speaking into the night. I could hear Finny's boots crunching against the gravel stones. My hand went to my chest as a sob began to rise in me. I felt the chain from my locket. I'd forgotten to take it off when I got home from the dance.

"Wait," I called out and Millie turned back toward me. Removing my silver locket, I placed it in Millie's hand and squeezed tight. "Give it to her...when she's old enough. Tell her..." I paused, swallowing back tears. "Tell her it's... tell her it's from a friend."

I pulled back the blanket and kissed Cammie's head one last time. Millie was right. If she stayed at the home, she'd surely die.

"I don't even know when her birthday is," said Millie.

I looked toward the waiting wagon. By the light of the moon I could see Jim Merry climb onto the wagon.

"December third," I said. "She was born in December."

We said very little on the way back to East Chester. Finny pulled into the driveway and parked.

"Do you think she'll be okay?" I couldn't stop wondering what the future would hold for Cammie.

"Better than if she stayed." I knew Finny was right; the maternity home was no place for Cammie. It was no place for any baby. Knowing all that, I was still going to miss her something fierce.

"I'm heading off tomorrow," said Finny as a moment of awkward silence passed between us.

"But...." There seemed no point. There was nothing I could say that would change his mind. I'd tried and tried. "You keep yourself safe, Finny Paul." It was all I could think to say.

He walked away, his silhouette fading into the night. An empty knot formed inside me as I watched Finny leave. He turned quickly and ran back. A spark of hope exploded in me. It wasn't too late for him to change his mind.

"Goodbye, Tulia," he said and then kissed me on the cheek. He turned again and raced down the driveway and then back onto the road.

I lay in bed that night looking out my window at the stars, wondering how far you'd have to travel before you came to the end and what the end would actually look like. My thoughts kept moving back and forth from Finny to Cammie. I would miss them both. I finally turned over and reached for my scrapbook but stopped. This wasn't something the scrapbook could make better. Pulling the quilt around me, I settled down into bed. The secret I was holding in my heart caused a dull ache in my chest. Finny knew my secret, but he was going away. There was no one else I could trust. Again, I thought about the night in November when we heard Becky crying out in pain.

"There were two babies, Tulia—a boy *and* a girl." Becky looked pale and tired. I almost cried when I saw her. I hadn't seen her since that day outside the maternity home when I tried convincing her to keep her baby. Back then, it seemed a simple solution. I should have known better. Becky always did know her own mind.

"Twins?" I croaked. "But why didn't Mrs. Young say?" It seemed almost impossible and yet Becky wouldn't make something like that up.

"The little girl is gone already. There was a family from Massachusetts. Mrs. Young said they were so happy to have her." Becky was smiling, but it wasn't a happy smile.

"What did she look like?" I whispered. Tears were pushing against the backs of my eyes.

"I didn't see her, Tulia—either one of them. Mrs. Young said it would be easier that way." Becky squeezed my hand. "Don't be sad. Everything will be fine, you'll see." She sat up in bed. She wiped away a tear that had formed under my right eye. "I'm going back to work, Tulia. I've made up my mind. I'm going to sign up and go overseas. They need nurses." I thought about what Ma had said, about Becky moving on with her life.

"Ma took the little boy to Tanner." I didn't know what else to say. I didn't want to think about Becky going overseas any more than I wanted to think about the little niece I'd never ever see.

"The Merrys will be happy," she said with a faint smile.

It made me wonder if for every person who was made happy by something, there was someone who was left equally unhappy.

# Epilogue

The aunties used to say the birthmark Becky had on the back of her neck had been left behind when the stork delivered her. They also said the mark, in the shape of angel wings, was a sign that Becky would receive every advantage the world had to offer. Becky was the only one of Ma's babies born with a stork bite at the nape of her neck, but the aunties insisted that it was a Thompson trait passed down for generations.

I grew up thinking that Becky would forever be protected from the harshness of life while the rest of us would remain at the mercy of fate. The rest of the family considered Becky lucky except for Ma, who passed the story off as an old wives' tale.

"There's no such thing as luck—good or bad," she'd say.

If the summer Becky came home pregnant proved anything to me, it was that the aunties had been wrong.

Becky wasn't favoured by the angels any more than the rest of us.

Mrs. Young was used to making last-minute arrangements when it came to burials and adoptions. Babies were often whisked away hours after they were born. I'd hear about a birth only to find no newborn in the nursery the next day. If anyone knew, they never said what happened. So while Ma was delivering the promised baby boy to the Merrys, Mrs. Young was sending the girl to Massachusetts, or so she said.

"What gives her the right to play God?" Finny Paul used to say. It took a while for me to accept that he was right. I cried many nights for my little niece and the nephew I'd only ever get to see from a distance. With no one in the family knowing, it would be as if neither of them ever existed. Ma was quiet when she came back from delivering the baby to the Merrys' open arms that day. We didn't even mention Becky's baby girl.

And then, almost miraculously, I found a baby in the nursery when I went out to help Ma with the laundry that next Saturday—someone to take the place of the little niece who was lost to the States, or so I thought. I wasn't sure whose baby she was and I didn't care that she wasn't what Mrs. Young would call perfect. In those few moments that I held her, my heart felt full. Her name suddenly came to me, like the whispers from an angel—Cammie. It fit her perfectly. I went back down to the laundry feeling lighter than I had since the night Becky's babies were born.

It was Sally who discovered the strange markings on the back of Cammie's neck while giving her a bath.

"Look at this," she said when I entered the nursery that day. "She has a birthmark."

"It's a stork bite," I said, recognizing it immediately. "Some people call them angel wings."

"Angel wings...I like that," said Sally, smiling.


As time went by, I came to see that the truth is not always as clear-cut as it might seem. Becky and Ma believed that Becky's baby girl had been adopted by a couple from Massachusetts. They had no reason not to; after all, it's what Mrs. Young told them. But I knew it that day in the nursery when I saw the angel wings on Cammie's neck that Mrs. Young had lied. Maybe she thought she was doing what was right by letting everyone think the baby was living a wonderful life in the States. Maybe in her mind that was better than telling Becky her baby was defective and no one would ever adopt her. Or maybe Finny Paul was right all those times he said Mrs. Young liked to play God, that she arranged other people's lives to suit herself. But God would never have let babies starve to death, especially ones that were weaker than the rest, and then bury them in butterboxes the way Mrs. Young did.

The aunties may have been wrong about the angel wings protecting Becky from harm, but they were right when they said that it was a Thompson trait. Becky was the only one of my sisters and brothers born with a stork bite, but many of my nieces and nephews had one. Like the aunties said, these things sometimes skip a generation.

As I lay in bed the night after Millie and Cammie left, I couldn't help thinking how unfair life could be. Drifting into sleep, I wondered if I'd done the right thing. But then I thought about how life doesn't offer guarantees. We do the best we can and hope things work out well. It's all we can do. And then I thought about the part I played in all of this. I had no idea what kind of life Millie would give Cammie. But I understood that sometimes you do things not because they're the right thing to do; you do them because sometimes you have no other choice.

# Author's Note

The Ideal Maternity Home is a tragic story that has been described as a dark chapter in Nova Scotia's history. The Home was in operation from the late 1920s until 1947, and was located in East Chester, Nova Scotia. It was run by Lila Young, a midwife, and William Young, a chiropractor. Local married couples came to the Home to have their babies. But it was also a place where unwed mothers could come to discreetly give birth and have adoptions arranged for their babies.

In the beginning, the Home was quiet and small but as time went on, and the business began to grow, it was increased to fifty-four rooms and fourteen bathrooms. Many of the babies were adopted by couples in the United States.

Soon, allegations of wrongdoing at the home began to circulate. And the Youngs' practices became more and more corrupt as time went on. In some cases, married couples who came to the Ideal Maternity Home to have their babies were told that their baby had died when really, the baby had been adopted out without their knowledge. It is also said that those babies who were considered unadoptable, either for the colour of their skin or because of birth defects, were fed only water and molasses and left to die. The babies who died were buried in small wooden boxes, or butterboxes, from the local creamery in the woods behind the Home or dumped into the ocean. This is where the term "Butterbox Babies" comes from.

It is estimated that between four and six hundred babies died at the home. There are survivors of the Ideal Maternity Home still searching for their birth families today.

# Acknowledgements

I am grateful to the many people who helped bring another Cammie book into the world. My thanks to the team at Nimbus Publishing and Vagrant Press for all your hard work and dedication.

My thanks to Penelope Jackson for guiding me through the edits of yet another book. Your insights and encouragement are always welcome.

Thank you to Whitney Moran for your enthusiasm for this book and for bringing it all together. You are great to work with.

I am grateful to Bette Cahill whose book, *Butterbox Babies*, provided valuable insights into life at the Ideal Maternity Home. Thank you for uncovering the truth of a story that remained a secret for far too long.

As always, I am grateful to all the people in my life who continue to support me through this writing journey of mine. Thanks for understanding how important this is to me, for your endless encouragement, interest, and enthusiasm for the stories I write.

Finally, my thoughts go out to all the survivors of the Ideal Maternity Home, especially to those still searching for their birth families. May you find the conclusion you're searching for.

SHELLEY ZINCK

**LAURA BEST** has had over forty short stories published in literary magazines and anthologies. Her first young adult novel, *Bitter, Sweet*, was shortlisted for the Geoffrey Bilson Award for Historical Fiction for Young People. The first book in the Cammie series, *Flying with a Broken Wing*, was named one of Bank Street College of Education's Best Books of 2015. Her most recent middle grade book, *Cammie Takes Flight*, the next in the series, was nominated for the 2018 Silver Birch Award. Her first novel for adults, *Good Mothers Don't*, was published in 2020. Her next middle-grade novel, *A Sure Cure For Witchcraft*, will be released in Fall 2021. She lives in East Dalhousie, Nova Scotia, with her husband, Brian. Visit lauraabest.wordpress.com.